The Stepsisters

#3

Bad Sisters

SCHOLASTIC INC.
New York Toronto London Auckland Sydney

No part of this publication may be reproduced in whole or in part, or stored in a retrieval system, or transmitted in any form or by any means, electronic, mechanical, photocopying, recording, or otherwise, without written permission of the publisher. For information regarding permission, write to Scholastic Inc., 730 Broadway, New York, NY 10003.

ISBN 0-590-40998-0

12 11 10 9 8 7 6 5 4 3 2 1   7 8 9/8 0 1 2/9

Printed in the U.S.A.   01

First Scholastic printing, December 1987

The Stepsisters

Bad Sisters

CHAPTER 1

With less than a minute to go, the ball changed hands. Paige Whitman rose with the others in the crowded press box as the blue and gold of her high school basketball team flowed down court for a last scoring goal. The buzzer blasted the air. The game was over. The boy at Paige's side groaned and fell back in his seat. "Eighty-eight to twenty-four," he wailed. "That was more like a track meet than a basketball game."

Paige flipped her long, dark hair back from her face and grinned. "Somebody always has to lose," she reminded him.

He shook his head. "You must be some kind of a witch, Whitman. Your school hasn't lost a game or a meet since you started covering sports with Ben Collins."

"Somebody has to win, too!" she told him, straining on tiptoe to look for Ben on a court suddenly filled with fans. In anything but a crowd of basketball players, her tall, rangy editor stuck out like a flag pole. But she knew where to look. Ben, the best high school photographer in Philadelphia, was always where the action was. When she located him, he was still snapping the pictures that would run with her story.

She worked her way through the crowd toward Ben. She was a tall, willowy brunette whose fine dark eyes shone with pleasure. If anyone had told Paige Whitman six months before that she would become a sports fan, she would have laughed. But then again, if they had told her that she would have a job on the staff of the school paper, she wouldn't have believed that either.

But the greatest astonishment of all was how much she cared about Ben. Before she met him, she had been hopelessly in love with Jake Carson for what seemed like forever. Even after her beautiful fifteen-year-old stepsister Katie had started going with Jake, Paige had still carried the torch for him.

Then she had met Ben. He was now so special to her that just seeing him like that, crouched a little with his eyes glued to his camera, quickened her steps.

When Ben lowered his camera for a moment, he saw Paige and motioned her toward the hall outside the gym. She nodded and let herself be carried through the door with the crowd to wait for him. The fans passed her, grumbling at the home team's defeat and bad-mouthing the coaching. Paige barely listened. Losers always found *something* to blame a defeat on.

The crowd had thinned when Ben appeared in

the door and started toward her. As he drew near, two heavyset young men stopped nearby to pull on their jackets.

"They ought to kick that bunch out of the conference," one of them fumed. "Nobody's got a chance against them the rotten way they cheat on qualifying athletes."

Paige felt Ben stiffen at her side. "Hold it!" he said roughly. "What are you talking about? Name me one man on this team who didn't qualify fairly."

The speaker flushed, glanced at Paige, then quickly looked away. "Okay," he said defensively. "So I don't know the basketball guys. But the way you cut corners on that swim team makes a guy wonder about everybody wearing your colors."

Swim team. Paige stared at him, aghast. Katie Summer, her stepsister Katie, was one of the real winners on that swim team. Ben's reaction was as instantaneous as her own, only angrier.

"You better bring a charge like that up front or keep your mouth shut," Ben warned him. "You could have a libel problem there."

"Who can prove anything?" the guy sneered. "But you find me anybody who believes your hot-shot swimming star is making the grades and I'll *eat* your camera."

Paige, knowing Ben's quick temper, held her breath.

"Quit it," Ben said coldly. "Name names or shut up."

The boy flushed a deep red. "How about Mike Lynch for starters?"

Paige felt herself go weak with relief. At least he wasn't accusing Katie. But Mike Lynch was one of Katie's best friends on the team. And Mike was a star, the fastest speed swimmer in the conference.

"Come on," the accuser's companion said, shoving him along. "You're wasting your time. They're not going to blow the whistle on a guy who could help them make All Conference."

Ben started to follow them, but Paige laid her hand on his arm. He stopped without even looking at her. "Mike Lynch," he whispered aloud to himself. "Have you heard anything about this before, Paige?"

She shook her head. "They're just mad because their team got beaten so badly."

"I don't think so," Ben said quietly. "Why would he bring up a swimmer at a basketball game, unless he'd heard something about Mike Lynch? He didn't pick that out of the air." He took Paige's hand and started off briskly. "Come on. We've got some thinking to do."

As much as she enjoyed the games, Paige looked forward even more to her time with Ben afterward. They always went to their favorite hangout, the crowded little Gem cafe that didn't serve anything but hamburgers, coffee, and cold sodas.

That night was different. Morose and silent, Ben strode in the opposite direction to a coffee shop which was as quiet as the Gem was noisy. He ordered coffee and then stared at the mug a long time before speaking.

When he took off his glasses and laid them on

4

the table, Paige knew he had made a decision. "Okay, Paige," he said, reaching over for her hand. "We take steps. We get to the bottom of this, and fast."

"How are we going to do that?" she asked, feeling frightened.

His expression turned to determination. "We investigate. That's what reporting is all about."

"But, Ben," Paige protested. "Remember me? I'm the lawyer's daughter. A person is innocent until proven guilty."

"I'll buy that only after we check it out thoroughly. We'll either prove that bimbo is wrong or we'll blow the whistle ourselves, as he so originally put it. And you're the one who gets to do it for us."

"Ben!" she wailed. "I don't know where to start. I'm not an investigator, *especially* if it involves the swim team." She thought of Katie with sudden panic.

"Come on, Paige," Ben scoffed. "You're a junior, you've been around a long time and know a lot of people. Talk to people who have classes with Mike Lynch. They'll know if he's not making the grades to swim on the team."

Paige shook her head firmly. "Anybody but me, Ben, please! Remember who else is on that team!"

She shouldn't have to remind him. He knew better than almost anyone how much trouble there had been between her and Katie. He had seen Paige's jealousy and the bad feelings between the two stepsisters almost ruin her life. "Ben, I can't."

"Paige," he said sternly. "Grow up! Katie's mother and your dad are married. We're talking forever here. Put your own feelings aside and be a good reporter. That's what you're not paid to be, right?"

Paige tried to return his smile but couldn't. Why couldn't anybody realize how tough it had been for her since her father's marriage? Couldn't they see that having to share your father, your home, even your own bedroom with a girl you couldn't stand was just horrible? She flushed at the knowledge that her pain only looked petty and childish to him.

"Look, Paige," Ben said, laying a tip on the table and reaching for her coat. "We're not talking about what you *want* to do, but what you *have* to do. If you're going to be a pro, you don't pick or choose what assignment you take. This story is being assigned to you, and I expect you to do it. Okay?"

Paige only nodded, not able to meet his eyes.

Katie Guthrie stood under the shower in the locker room a long time, letting the hot water stream over her smooth body and soothe the muscles which were sore from her arduous swimming workout. But the practice had been good. And glory! She had held her record speed for the third time in a row.

She hummed to herself as she buffed herself dry. When her mother married Bill Whitman and moved the family, Katie and her older brother Tuck and younger sister Mary Emily, from Atlanta to Philadelphia, Katie had desperately hoped she could qualify to swim on the team of her new, larger high school. That dream had come true.

How confident she had been that her new life would be completely exciting. She would adore her new home and new family, and have loads of cool new friends. She certainly had great friends . . . Sara and Lisa were just wonderful to be with! She didn't mind the big old Victorian house at all, except for having to share a bedroom with Paige. As for excitement! There was Jake Carson, the most attractive and somehow mysterious boy she had ever known.

And she would see him tonight!

She hugged herself in the towel. The only thing she could really complain about was her stepsister Paige. Katie paused, frowning. Twice in the few months since the move, Paige had deliberately gone out of her way to make deep trouble for Katie. She would just have to be careful, that was all. She must never trust Paige for a single moment about *anything!*

Katie had finished dressing but was combing her hair in front of the mirror when somebody banged on the door, shouting her name. She glanced at the mirror one last time and smiled at herself. Her thick fair hair, nearly dry, curled loosely on her shoulders, and she didn't really need even a touch of makeup with her skin rosy from her swim. Her blue eyes were bright in her lovely face.

She thought resentfully of how Paige clearly thought Katie was conceited about her looks. Was there any crime in *liking* how you look?

7

When the banging started again, Katie opened the door swiftly. Mike Lynch, the star speed swimmer on the team, stood in the hall looking as happy and full of energy as Katie herself felt. Mike was tall for a swimmer and his broad shoulders gave him a solid, powerful look. His hair was still wet, giving his broad grin a framework of damp curls.

"Hey, beautiful," he said. "I was ready to send in troops. Want a ride home?"

She smiled up at him. What a nice guy, and what a swimmer! "You know me! I never turn down a really good offer."

"Don't give me that," he laughed. "How many times have I asked you out and gotten nowhere?"

"I've no head for numbers," Katie said airily. "Someday maybe I'll surprise you."

"And I'll probably drop dead," he told her, reaching ahead of her to shove the door open.

Mike kidded her on the way home. "Without pushing my luck, any chance of your seeing a movie with me this weekend?"

"I really am sorry, Mike," Katie told him. "You know I go out with Jake Carson pretty steadily."

"Maybe *he's* the one who should be surprised," Mike muttered, pulling up in front of the Whitman house. Lights already glowed from the long windows, spilling across the porch. The fancy carved trim on the fine old house shone in the last light of afternoon. A car stood in the drive, which explained why the Whitman's dog Scarlett was barking up a storm from the backyard.

"Oh, oh," Mike said quietly. "Speak of the unwanted."

8

Katie turned to see Jake Carson standing beside his car in the drive, staring at them. "I don't talk that way about your friends," she rebuked Mike. "But thanks a ton for the ride, Mike."

"There's more where that came from," Mike told her hopefully.

Katie was quickly up the walk and at Jake's side.

"Hey," she said warmly, looking up at him. "I didn't expect you, but it's a treat anyway!" It was always a treat to see Jake. In fact, it was a treat just to look at him. She had loved the way he looked from the very first. Back then, she had thought of almost legendary people, Rhett Butler maybe, or Heathcliff. Now he was Jake himself, which was even better — the dark, intense eyes, the handsome molding of his face. As usual, his expression was solemn, but awfully appealing.

"Obviously, you didn't expect me," he said coldly. "I guess that was Mike Lynch out in the car."

She nodded. "He gave me a ride home."

"Always Lynch, isn't it?"

"Jake! He's my friend. And we get out of swim practice at the same time."

"Sure, Katie," Jake said with a hint of sarcasm. Then he frowned and checked his watch. "I hate to do this, but I have to break our date tonight. I have a problem."

Katie studied him, waiting. She and Jake had had a few problems, but she thought they were in the past. "You could have called," she suggested, when he still didn't speak.

"I wanted to explain in person. You remember

my friend Gary? We went to a party at his house."

She nodded. "I remember Gary very well." She remembered his girlfriend, too, and all Jake's other friends who had treated her like a child once they realized she was only fifteen. That evening, one of the most miserable in her life, had ended with her and Jake breaking up for too long a time.

"Gary's in the hospital. Woke up sick this morning and had to have an emergency appendectomy."

"That's awful!" Katie said. "Can we go see him? Take him something . . . candy, magazines?"

"Maybe later," Jake said. "The problem is that team he coaches. Remember, girls' basketball? Somebody has to fill in for him until the season is over, or he's able to move around out there. I'm elected."

Katie grinned in spite of herself. "Why is it hard for me to imagine you a coach instead of a lawyer?"

"Because I'm not a lawyer yet, and I've never coached anything before. But I have played a lot of basketball. There's a game tonight, that's why I have to cancel the date. Unfortunately, there'll be a lot of games in the next few weeks."

"Can't I go with you?"

He looked at her thoughtfully and shook his head. "I don't think that would work." He took her hand and grinned at her. "You're too distracting. But we'll make it up later. You do understand?"

There went the evening she had looked forward to all week! She forced a smile. "I understand that I'll miss you, Jake."

He took her suddenly by the shoulders. His kiss was as sudden and swift as it was demanding. "That's two of us, Katie," he said, his voice suddenly husky. Then he pulled away and muttered. "Gotta run! I'll call you!"

Katie watched him drive away. Jake would never know how much she looked forward to her time with him. And his doubt that they were right for each other would always keep her from telling him as often as she'd like to.

Katie's mind was still on Jake as she let herself into the kitchen. Paige, who was standing in front of the refrigerator, glanced over her shoulder.

"Finally tore yourself away?" she asked sarcastically.

Katie fought a sudden rise of fury. Why couldn't she ever have a minute of privacy around this place? The thought that Paige had been watching her and Jake from the window made her burn. She put on her brightest, most sparkling smile. "Tear myself away?" she asked. "Paige, how can you *always* get things messed up? Jake was tearing himself away from *me*. Or didn't you know that was how it worked?"

Paige stared at her, her face reddening, before slamming the refrigerator door and stalking out of the room.

Katie heard her going up the stairs and sighed. Now Katie didn't dare go up to change unless she wanted to confront Paige again. Paige would be waiting there in the middle of all the mess she strewed around the room, waiting to take another dig at her. Paige wasn't swift on the comeback, but she cut deep when she did say anything. And since their last run-in, Paige hadn't said two words to her in public. But she hadn't said a civil one to her in private either.

And it was painful enough to know that she and Jake would have so little time together for a while.

CHAPTER 2

One of the things Paige Whitman loved about working on the newspaper was the atmosphere of the office itself. It was a crazy place with phones jangling and the typewriters clattering constantly. Ben paced back and forth on his long legs when anything excited or upset him. More often than not he *was* excited and therefore shouting, with Laurie Harris, his co-editor, yelling right back at him. Going there after classes had always been like walking onto the set of a TV sitcom, where Paige had a ringside seat and a bit part of her own.

Suddenly, she had more than a minor part in the drama. The whole atmosphere changed because of Paige's quiet investigation of the rumor that Mike Lynch wasn't really making the grades to qualify for the swim team. Ben was restlessly impatient for results, and the rest of the staff, Jim Gordon and Carrie Moffat, as well as Laurie, realized the importance of the story and how much harm it could do the school if the rumor proved to be true.

Paige had to look down physically on Laurie, who wasn't much taller than Paige's ten year old sister and stepsister. But she didn't look down on her any other way. Laurie, her broad freckled face twisted with thought, listened to Paige stumble out her fear of taking on the swim team story.

"Laurie, you can't imagine how important swimming is to my stepsister. Katie keeps herself on a special diet, she always gets to bed on time. For me to get involved in something that important to her scares me. Especially if the rumor should turn out to be true and the swim team is in trouble."

"And you two don't get along, do you?" Laurie asked thoughtfully.

Paige shook her head. "We haven't from the first day. We're just so different." Paige felt herself flush. "And I've done some dumb things that have made it very tough at home."

Laurie sighed. "One sure thing, you aren't going to change Ben's mind."

"And I don't even know how to start!" Paige said.

Laurie chewed her lip in thought, then grinned. "Carefully. Get the class lists for Mike's schedule. Tell the office anything you want to. They'll think we need it for the paper. Look through the lists and find people you can talk to. Be sure it's somebody you trust not to go blabbing around that you're asking questions about Mike Lynch. Kids know how other kids are doing in their classes. Maybe they'll even mention Mike's special friends. If he's getting help, somebody knows who's helping. But be careful. If we're wrong, we could be in trouble."

Carrie Moffat, who covered the student council, glanced up. "Lynch is in my third-hour English class," she told Paige. "What do you want to know?"

"Just anything you can tell me about his performance, I guess," Paige told her.

Carrie pulled a sheet out of her typewriter impatiently and scoffed. "Performance! How about a male Sleeping Beauty? He slumps in a chair back in the corner with his eyes at half-mast."

"But isn't there a lot of discussion in an English class?" Paige asked.

Carrie nodded. "But you know how that is. The kids who choose to sit up front and down the middle of the room beat everyone else with answers."

"Does he not know what's going on?"

Carrie shrugged. "Who knows? He never opens his mouth. But he must be passing the tests and getting his themes in on time or Mr. Zuber would put his name on the hit list."

"Hit list?" Jim asked, looking up without missing a beat on his typewriter.

"Zuber's little joke," Carrie explained. "He writes the names of students falling behind up in the corner of the front board. Above it is a sign: HIT THE BOOKS OR HIT THE ROAD."

"Hey," Laurie grinned. "I like that. We should be able to use it in the paper sometime . . . without the current names, of course."

Mike's daily schedule was easy to get. After that, it was only a matter of putting the class lists into the copier one at a time until she had a full set.

Ben wasn't being fair to her. Sure she knew a lot of people, but you don't just go up to a senior and start quizzing him about a classmate, especially not one as popular as Mike Lynch. She was glad to see Alex Moore's name on the senior chemistry list. That made sense. Alex was a star student, always had been, and fortunately was also an old friend. Nervous about having the lists, Paige folded them in an envelope in the back flap of her notebook and waited for a chance to talk to Alex alone.

Lunch was Katie's favorite hour of the school day. It wasn't that she was that crazy about food, it was just the only time when she and her crowd of friends could get together and talk. They were all there when Katie flew into the cafeteria wearing her new electric blue jacket over a pleated white skirt.

Lisa Conrad, looking her usual dramatic self with her coal-black hair tumbling onto the shoulders of a brilliant red shaker knit sweater, looked up and laughed.

"What's with you, Katie? You've worn that jacket three days in a row. Is it your new uniform?"

"It's a campaign I'm waging against my mother.

16

This is the only really stylish thing she's let me buy since we got here. I intend to wear it until she's so sick of it, she pops for more new clothes."

Trish Harrison and Diane Powers both laughed. "That might work better if it didn't look so good on you," Trish said.

Sara Nolan grinned. "I could lend you something," she offered in an innocent tone.

Katie laughed along with the others. They all remembered when she had tried that. Sara's outfit had reduced her mother to name-calling, but in the end Virginia Mae had given in and let her buy the jacket and a pair of short red boots.

"I'm glad I didn't take the pizza," Nickie Myers said, looking at Katie's tossed salad and whole wheat bun. "I don't know why your ears don't grow like a rabbit's with all the green stuff you munch."

"We athletes. . ." Katie said lightly. "Listen. Is anything cool going on this weekend? If so, count me in."

Sara turned her heart-shaped face toward Katie in astonishment. "Don't tell me something has happened between you and Tall, Dark, and Inscrutable."

Katie laughed. "I wish you wouldn't call Jake that, even if he is. No problem, really. He's just filling in for a friend and won't have much time for a while. A weekend in the house with Paige Whitman can seem like an eternity."

"I'm at loose ends, too," Lisa told her. "How about a bunch of us doing a movie downtown and going for pizza," she paused and grinned at Katie, "or a salad, of course, afterward."

Sara and Diane nodded, but Nickie frowned. "What kind of job is this that keeps Jake out at night?"

"Coaching," Katie told her. "His friend Gary Ames is sick and Jake is taking over Gary's girls' basketball team."

Trish whistled softly. "For anybody, but you, that would be murder."

"What do you mean?" Katie asked.

"Where's your head? I wouldn't want my guy hanging out with ten or twelve knockout girl athletes. Like I said, none of them are as cool as you are, but there's still a lot of exposure."

"In those little tiny short shorts, too," Sara added.

Katie grinned at them. "Lay off! The last thing I need is a good case of jealousy. Green eyes wouldn't match my only jacket! Right?"

"It must be great to feel so secure," Diane sighed, rising just as the bell sounded. "Back to the wars!"

Twice during her next class Katie found herself remembering Trish's words. She hadn't even thought about Jake being attracted to any of those girls. For one thing he was older. He had already graduated and was just taking off a year before starting the long haul of college and then law school. He wouldn't be interested in a bunch of high school girls. She gasped at her own thought. But I'm only a *sophomore* in high school, she reminded herself. And he got interested in me fast enough!

This was all she needed, to not see Jake and worry about new competition at the same time!

18

* * *

Paige took a chance and looked for Alex Moore in the library after school, before even checking in at the newspaper office. Her guess paid off. She saw Alex from the door. His brown hair was touseled and his expression intense as he studied the titles along the reference shelf near the back of the library.

She walked over and stood beside him a moment before he noticed her. "Hi, Paige," he said, his voice warm.

The neat thing about Alex was that he was as pleasant to look at as he was nice. He was basically shy, had been clear back to when they were in junior high together. But clothes looked good on his tall, slender frame, and his eyes, such a deep blue that they looked black from a distance, were so level and open on her own that she instinctively smiled. But now that she was with him, how could she start? Laurie had warned her to be careful.

"How are things going, Alex?" she asked.

His expression looked puzzled. "Fine, how about you?"

"I'm fine, too," she said, knowing how awkward this had suddenly become. "But then I'm not in any senior science courses like my brainy friend."

"Come off it." Alex laughed. "It isn't all that tough."

This was getting nowhere. She had no choice but to take the plunge. "Isn't Mike Lynch in that class with you?"

He looked at her steadily a moment, then

smiled. "So it's gotten around to you, too? I've never heard such a whispering campaign against a guy."

"I've heard it," Paige nodded. "Just really confidentially, Alex, do you think there's anything to it?"

He pulled down an armful of books and started toward the table where he had left his notebook and jacket. "Paige, I'd really rather not talk to you about it."

She followed him, confused. "But Alex!" she protested, taking the chair across from him, "I'm not going to quote you to anybody."

He opened his notebook and stared at it a long time. "I know that, Paige, but that's not the problem. I hate this kind of stuff," he said with sudden anger. "I hate gossip. I hate the idea of kids cheating in school, and I especially hate it when it's a guy like Mike, who could do the work if he wasn't so lazy."

When she said nothing, he spoke quietly without looking up at her. "That's not the worst. Look, Paige, after that rotten thing you did with the picture of Katie Guthrie in the swim team article, everybody knows you two don't get along."

Paige felt herself choking. "It *was* rotten of me to get that awful picture published, Alex. It was a crazy impulse I gave in to and have to live with. But it's over."

"Nothing's ever over, Paige, you know that!" he corrected her. "But because I know how you feel about your stepsister, I'd really rather not talk to you about Mike Lynch."

Paige stared at him. This didn't make sense.

"But nobody has accused *Katie* of cheating."

His expression gave him away. Paige felt her heart drop down around her knees somewhere. When she spoke, her voice came out in a terrified whisper. "Oh, no, Alex."

His eyes were full of instant sympathy. "Why did I have to say that? But it's out, I guess. It's all over school that Katie is the one who's doing the work for him, his papers, helping with tests I guess. He sure isn't making it on daily class work."

Paige looked at him silently. Ben had to take her off this assignment. It was bad enough for her to snoop around Katie's swim team; it was something else if Katie was supposed to be involved in the scandal. Paige wondered if this could be true. Or could some jealous person have started the whole thing to hurt Katie?

Would Katie have helped Mike? I wouldn't put anything past her, Paige thought.

"Alex," Paige asked swiftly, "just one more thing. Where did you hear this? Do you have any idea where this rumor started?"

He shook his head. "Who knows where rumors start, Paige? It only takes one loudmouth to launch a scandal. Why shouldn't people jump to the conclusion that it's Katie? Everybody knows what good friends Katie and Mike are. Everybody knows how important the ranking of that swim team is to both of them . . . Katie as much as Mike. It's all over school. I'm amazed you haven't heard it before now." He shrugged. "Hey, Paige, be realistic! Everybody who has a class with Mike Lynch knows he hasn't cracked a book all year."

"But that doesn't mean Katie's involved," Paige said, trying to be rational.

"She's the one who hangs out with him the most. They don't date, but she rides home with him a lot. Watch them; you can tell how much they like each other. And they *are* the stars of that team, you know. Paige, I really *am* sorry."

Paige sat silent for a moment. "I'm sorry, too, Alex," she finally said, rising. "But thanks a lot. You really have helped."

"Yeah," he said with a note of irony. "I just bet I have!"

Paige left the library with her head spinning. Alex had made a good case. In a way she hoped he was right about Katie. It was certainly time for Katie to get hers. For a change, nobody could blame Paige for feeling that way. The thought left swiftly, leaving both guilt and fear. It was awful to hope that Katie was cheating, but Paige was going to get blamed plenty when the story hit print.

Paige's first impulse was to go straight back to the newspaper office and *make* Ben take her off the story. If he won't, I'll quit, she promised herself. But even as she thought it, she knew she wouldn't. She loved the work and being part of the excitement. But most of all, she knew Ben would say that what she had heard was all the more reason she should stay on the story.

Ben looked up instantly when she walked into the office a half hour late. "Anything new?" he asked.

She nodded. "Nothing big. Just that the story is all over, coming from every direction, and that

Mike Lynch is definitely getting help somewhere."

"You're keeping on it?" Ben asked.

She nodded. He hadn't asked if she had heard anything about this "somewhere" and she didn't have the nerve to tell him. "But not because I want to," she reminded him.

Katie knew Jake would be working that afternoon at the Whitman house when she accepted the ride home with Mike Lynch. She had thought about what Trish had said all day and decided that she needed to be up front with Jake about her friendship with Mike. If he could hang out with a bunch of neat-looking young athletes, she could accept a ride home from a friend.

When Katie first met Jake, she'd had a hard time realizing why Jake had taken a job doing anything as menial as yard work. He'd made super grades, starred in basketball, and came from an outstanding old Philadelphia family.

"I like hard work," Jake had told her. "Bill Whitman is one of the best attorneys in this town, and I really like the man."

"But why work at all, if you're only going back to school later?"

He had shaken his head at her. "Look, Katie, I come from a family with old Yankee ethics. A person works! I like paying my way, and I have a long way to go. I'm going to be a better attorney, maybe even a better judge, than my father and grandfather. You get places by working."

"The competition is already in place," Mike said glumly as he let Katie out in front of the house.

"You are my *friend*," Katie reminded him.

"My first ray of hope," he said, grinning at her. "If you're not friends with Carson, forget him!"

She laughed going up the walk. Crazy guy. Wasn't he ever going to give up?

"Well, hello, stranger," she told Jake, picking her way through his tools to where he was doing a carpentry job on the garage.

He only grunted and went on twisting a piece of wire.

"Look at you! All smiles and grins," she teased him. "What's the matter? Isn't your new job going well, coach?"

"The coaching is fine," he said without looking at her. "It just burns me to see you with Mike Lynch."

"Come on, Jake," Katie coaxed, but feeling annoyed. "He's a real fine athlete. We work together on the best high school swim team in the conference."

Jake turned and stared at her without smiling. "And I am coaching the best girls' basketball team in *our* conference," he told her. "How would you like my riding those girls around in my car?"

Katie felt her face flush with sudden color and could have kicked Trish for suggesting the whole business about Jake and the girls.

"What a lovely way you have of putting things." But then she added, "I'd hate it."

"Well?" Jake said lightly, walking away to go back into the garage.

Katie stood staring after him a moment, then ran into the house.

CHAPTER 3

Paige finished late at the newspaper office. By the time she reached the hill that led to her house, the streetlights were blinking on. She stood a long minute, looking up at the big yellow Victorian house that had been her home for the entire sixteen years of her life. From the outside, with warm lamplight streaming through the windows, it looked like every family's dream house.

Inside it probably looked the same way. Upstairs in their shared room, her little sister Megan and Mary Emily Guthrie were probably sitting cross-legged on the floor, playing a game together. The two younger girls had adored each other from the day they met and were the world's happiest stepsisters.

In the next room, Paige's seventeen-year-old stepbrother Tuck Guthrie would be studying, wearing his Walkman radio to drown out the younger girls' giggling. Coming into a new school as a senior and a southerner had been tough on Tuck. When he fell for Jennifer Bailey, life had improved. Even though Jennifer still dated the quarterback Ed Thomas who really had it in for Tuck, Jennifer and Tuck spent enough time together to keep Tuck's hopes high.

Paige's father's dream of the Whitman and Guthrie children joining into one big happy family had really worked out for everyone but Paige herself. Paige's stepmother, Virginia Mae, was obviously happy. Paige could imagine her at the piano in the study, her fingers drifting from one selection to another as she waited for all of them to come home.

Why me? Paige asked herself. Why do I have to be the only one the dream had turned sour for?

She had loved Virginia Mae from the start. Not only was her stepmother a beautiful and talented woman, but she was open and understanding, too. Paige always knew where she stood with Virginia Mae, which was more than she could say for her own father anymore. In fact, the only mysterious thing about Virginia Mae was that her first husband, Katie and Tuck and Mary Emily's father, had left her. Paige wondered guiltily if he had found his daughter Katie as impossible to live with as Paige did.

And here Katie was, making life impossible all over again. Paige's mind still reeled from what Alex had told her so reluctantly. More than anything she wished she didn't *ever* have to go inside that house again!

At the back of the house, the fragrance of a rich Italian sauce hit Paige even before she opened the door. She sniffed appreciatively as she stepped inside and put her books on the table. Miss Aggie, who had been with Paige's family even before Paige's mother died, turned to greet her.

"That smells fabulous," Paige told her. "I think I'll walk the dog before dinner."

Aggie frowned. "I think Tuck already took her out."

"It won't hurt her to go twice," Paige said, pulling down the leash and letting herself out the back door.

Paige crossed the street with Scarlett bounding at her side. Once in the park, she found a bench and snapped off the dog's leash to let her run. Paige shivered as much from the problem she was facing as from the chill of the concrete bench.

She was scared.

More than that, she was hurt, too.

Why did somebody she liked so much have to put her into this no-win situation?

And she *couldn't* win. There was absolutely no way.

Twice since her father's marriage the summer before she had lost control of her anger at Katie. Both times she had struck out on impulse, although she wasn't a person who usually did things like that! Both times her father had been furious. After all those years of their being such a close warm team, her father no longer trusted her. He had as much as told her that although he loved her (as if it were a duty), he didn't really *like* her any more.

This last blow-up, over putting an ugly picture of Katie in the school paper, had been the worst.

She had promised both her father and herself that she would play straight with Katie no matter how mad she got or how tempted she was.

She didn't dare break her promise to her father or to herself, but what was she going to do about Ben? Ben wasn't patient. Ben wasn't going to be put off very long. Sooner or later she had to tell him that Katie was the one everyone suspected. Then Paige herself would be in trouble even though Katie started it. No way to win.

Scarlett returned to her knee, panting and looking up for approval. As Paige absently stroked the dog's head, Scarlett twisted and whined. Following her eyes, Paige saw her father's car turn into the drive.

When Alex had first told her about Katie's involvement in Mike Lynch's cheating, a big part of Paige had resisted believing him. But the more she thought about it, the more convinced she was that Katie really *was* the logical culprit.

Paige's list of reasons kept growing.

She knew how important the team standing was to Katie. She knew what good friends Katie and Mike Lynch were. Katie herself had been on academic probation early in the year. She knew better than anyone how awful it was to be kept from what you wanted to do because of grades.

But Paige was still amazed that Katie would do anything that completely stupid. Katie sparkled and laughed and flirted constantly, but she wasn't anything like the dumb, beautiful blonde she sometimes pretended to be. Katie's glowing golden curls hid a good, functional brain.

Maybe Katie just thought of it as helping a

friend. Maybe she hadn't even thought through to what would happen when the truth came out. Paige sighed again and forced herself to take the dog back home.

The meal which had smelled so delicious, tasted so much like cardboard in Paige's mouth. She was so deep in her thoughts that her father spoke to her twice before she heard him. She looked up in nervous alarm to see him laughing at her.

"I offered you a penny for your thoughts, but I'll raise the bid," he said. "I don't think you've heard a word that's been said here tonight."

Paige blushed. "I'm sorry," she said quickly. "I guess I was a million miles away."

"Anything you'd like to share?" Virginia Mae asked.

Paige felt her color deepen. "Not really," she said. "It's not very interesting."

"*My* thoughts are worth at least *fifty* cents," Megan said quickly. "Payment in advance, of course."

Mary Emily giggled and Virginia Mae laughed softly. Paige's father didn't laugh. Paige felt his eyes on her, concerned and a little annoyed at her continuing silence. She excused herself and escaped upstairs as soon as she could.

Once at the door of her room, Paige paused before forcing herself to go in. The air would smell faintly of one of the expensive perfume samples that Katie kept in a ruffled basket on the dresser. Katie's bed would be neatly made with the fancy pillows piled high under the ribbon hung above it.

Katie called this her "memory" ribbon, a long

29

strip of heavy pink velvet with dance programs and dried corsages and valentines pinned the whole length. To Paige it looked more like a warrior's belt with the scalps of Katie's conquests out on display for the world to see.

The wide window overlooking the park was the dividing line that separated Paige's half of the room from Katie's. Even if Paige's bed had been made, her clothes picked up, and her shoes not out on the floor, you could tell which side of the room was hers. Shadow and sunshine, Paige's navy blue coverlet contrasting with Katie's floral bedspread; the closet turning from pinks and purples to sensible blues and greens at the dividing line in the center.

Paige threw herself on her bed and turned her face to the wall. All the years this had been her room alone, it had seemed big and comfortable. Now it felt cramped and airless, with her step-sister's hatred for her hanging in the air even when Katie was not in the room.

The next days were agony for Paige. Every one she talked to had heard the same rumor, that Katie Guthrie was keeping Mike's grades up to protect the team standing. Although Ben nagged at her constantly to bring the business to an end, she couldn't force herself to tell him what she was hearing.

Between Ben's pressure and her increasing nervousness at home, Paige felt awful, almost as if something was terribly wrong physically. She had trouble sleeping. Some nights when she lay across the room from Katie, listening to her step-sister's even breathing, she thought about confronting Katie with the rumor. She even rehearsed things she could say to Katie.

But if she did come right out and ask her, what would Katie do?

Paige winced at her own answer. Katie would go off like a fire cracker, calling her names, accusing her of bad motives, somehow getting everyone's sympathy, no matter how much Katie herself was in the wrong.

All this time Paige felt her father quietly watching her. In spite of her deliberate efforts to avoid him, he finally caught her alone. "You've been awfully quiet lately, Paige," he said. "What's the matter?"

She shrugged and tried to smile. "I'm not the chatterbox of the family," she reminded him. The minute it was out, she was sorry. He scowled a little, obviously taking this as another dig at Katie who really *was* a chatterbox.

"Don't you feel well?" Mr. Whitman asked, his tone colder.

"I'm not sick, if that's what you mean."

He flushed with anger. "Paige, I'm trying to help you, and I'm trying to be patient. You're not making it easy for me on either score. If you can't tell your own father what's bothering you, who *can* you tell?"

His words startled her.

The answer was "no one." She didn't even dare tell her best friend Judy Belnap, because Judy really *believed* that Paige was out to get her stepsister.

31

"If there was anything I *could* tell you, I would," Paige told her father.

"I hope this doesn't mean that you and Katie still haven't made up," he said. "I never see you two exchange two words."

"We don't always have that much to say to each other," Paige said.

Mr. Whitman sighed and rose. "Very well, Paige, but you know how I feel about your making a genuine effort to get along with Katie."

Paige nodded. She knew only too well.

When Katie got a phone call from Midge Anderson, it took her a minute to place the name. "We met at Gary Ames's house," Midge reminded her. "Remember the party?"

"Oh yes, Midge, of course," Katie said warily. Her mind moved swiftly. Why was Midge calling her? Midge certainly hadn't gone out of her way to be nice to Katie at Gary's party. In fact, you might even say Midge had gone out of her way to be rude and make Katie feel young and stupid. Midge was lucky Katie even admitted remembering her name after that night!

"You heard about Gary?" Midge asked.

"Jake told me," Katie replied coolly. "How's he getting along?"

Midge groaned. "Typical male animal! To hear him talk, you'd think he was dying. Actually, he's healing even better than expected. But he's driving me crazy."

Katie hesitated but had little choice but to be polite. "Anything I can do to help?" she asked.

Midge's low chuckle came over the phone.

"Thought you'd never ask! Gary thinks Jake is telling him good stuff about the team just to keep his spirits up. You and I know Jake better than that, but Gary is a worry-wart. They're in a practice game this afternoon. I thought maybe you'd like to come along. . . ."

Katie frowned. "I'm not sure Jake would like me to do that," she told Midge.

"I'm not sure he wants *me* spying on him either," Midge admitted, "But I'm not asking him. Anyway, it's a free country. But don't come along just for my sake. I thought you'd enjoy seeing Jake in action."

Katie was surprised Midge had asked her. But she answered, "I would. I'd like to go."

"Great!" Midge said and went on to make arrangements to pick Katie up. Katie set down the phone thoughtfully. Jake had said she would be a distraction. She could always ask Midge if they could sit where Jake wouldn't even notice them.

Fans were scattered through the bleachers in knots here and there. The game had obviously been going on for some time. Even from their seats halfway up the bleachers, Katie could see the players' faces and arms shine with sweat.

Jake ranged along the side of the court, a silver whistle bouncing against his dark shirt. He looked wonderfully handsome, but so different from the Jake she was used to that Katie stared in disbelief. His hair had fallen untidily in his face, which also shone with sweat, as if he had been out there running with the rest of them. And he was shouting. Jake shouting?

But the girls were the most overwhelming. They were all tall, some even taller than Jake. And beautiful. She remembered something about "Gary's lovelies" being mentioned by some boy the night of the party. Katie had wanted to tell him women athletes shouldn't be called anyone's "lovelies," but she hadn't. The expression hadn't suggested the vibrant, laughing young women she was watching. They were good and they were fast with long smooth legs and supple bodies that twisted gracefully away from the opposing guards and in under the hoop.

"These are *high school girls?*" Katie whispered to Midge.

Midge chuckled. "Tall, aren't they? Really knockout girls, all of them. Watch number seventeen over there. Her name's Sandy. You wouldn't believe the points she's racked up."

"I'd believe," Katie murmured, as number seventeen twisted her body into a flying leap and tipped the ball into the basket.

Why had she worried about Jake seeing her and Midge? He had eyes for no one but his team. Then the final whistle blew.

Katie had never seen Jake smile as much or as easily, nor look so completely delighted, as he did walking off court followed by that team of giant girls, laughing and dancing around him.

"Well, that's that!" Midge said, rising and stretching. "I can honestly report that the girls are doing their thing just as Jake reported." Midge paused and looked at Katie. "Want to wait around until he showers and see your guy? I'll wait for you. Look, Katie, I know I was witchy at Gary's party. I'm sorry. You're a nice kid."

Katie grinned at her. "Thanks, not for the 'kid' part, but thanks. You'll want to check in with Gary right away. A good spy turns in a fast report. And anyway, I need to get back home. But it was fun. Thanks for bringing me."

"You're a better sport than I am," Midge said as they got into her car. "The first time I saw those girls acting like Gary belonged to them, I nearly split with jealousy."

"It doesn't bother you any more?" Katie asked, hoping she wouldn't give away the pangs of jealousy she was having.

Midge grinned. "I just keep telling myself that they all smell like sweat and then go splash myself again with perfume I can't afford."

"I'll remember that line in case I need it," Katie told her. Just as if she didn't need it already!

Katie's stepfather looked up as she started through the hall. "Got a minute?" he asked.

She went to the living room door, still carrying her jacket. "At your service, sir!"

He grinned as he always did when she smiled at him. "I'm thinking seriously of brightening my social life by taking out some lovely young women," he said in a serious, confidential tone. Before Katie could catch her breath, he went on. "What I had in mind was to take a couple of them downtown for a fancy lunch this Saturday. You have to be one of them!"

Katie laughed. "You had me going there for a

minute. But I really am sorry. I've already planned to spend Saturday with Lisa and Sara. Are rain checks available for this posh event?"

His disappointment was obvious, but he nodded. "Rain checks are definitely available," he said. "Could you possibly hold next Saturday for me? I've already talked to Paige. I think it would be a good thing for the three of us to have some quiet social time together . . . to talk things out."

Katie nodded, but groaned inwardly. She had been asleep on her feet to walk right into that one. So Paige was the other lovely young woman. She could instantly name three things she would rather die than do:

Talk to Paige.

Talk things out with Paige.

Talk things out with Paige, when Paige's father was the only other person present.

CHAPTER 4

The high point of Tuck Guthrie's school day was always his English class. It wasn't that he was that caught up with *Moby Dick,* which the class was currently toiling through. English was special because Jennifer Bailey sat where he could look at her. Melville's white whale didn't have a running chance against a brown-eyed redhead like Jennifer. Tuck grinned with anticipation as he swung in through the door.

Jennifer had been the first, and so far was the only, girl in Philadelphia that really attracted him. As his stepsister Paige Whitman had pointed out right away, Jennifer was more than a knockout to look at, she was also bright, funny, and completely cool.

But Jennifer had been a challenge. She not only wore the letter sweater of the school's star quarterback Ed Thomas, but she hadn't dated anybody but Ed for a long time before Tuck came along.

Ed had tried the classic gorilla tactics, growling, threatening, even roughing Tuck up, to protect what he considered his territory.

Fortunately for Tuck, Ed's tactics hadn't worked. Jennifer had a mind of her own, and Tuck had no intention of being strong-armed out of anything as interesting as Jennifer.

But Tuck still saw a lot less of Jennifer than he wanted to. That made English class a daily bonus.

Jennifer had apparently been watching for him. She caught Tuck's eye and smiled up at him. Tuck gripped his books. A guy could get a sunburn from a smile with that many amps. He was still enjoying the reaction when he realized she was signaling him with a folded note.

He swerved to pass her desk. Looking down, he realized that in spite of the smile, her brown eyes were dark with concern as she pressed the note into his hand.

"I need to talk to you," the note read. "Can we meet after school?" He looked up and saw her watching, her expression very serious. When he nodded agreement, she turned back to face the front of the class, leaving him confused and concerned.

Now what was up?

Was Jennifer going to warn him, as she had once before, that Ed was out to get him? If that was the case, no problem. Ed might be bigger and more primitive, but he wasn't dealing with a wimp either.

But maybe she wanted to tell him it was all off between them. That *would* be serious.

What seemed like several hours later, the bell

finally rang. Jennifer was waiting in the hall. "Not to be eager or anything," he said, smiling down at her, "But what's up?"

It wasn't like Jennifer to be indecisive, but she dropped her eyes and hesitated. "Can we go somewhere? Have a Coke maybe?"

"Paddy's okay?" Tuck asked.

She nodded. "I'll dump my stuff and meet you at the door."

Usually the smell of charcoal brought Tuck instant starvation. He didn't even notice it as he led Jennifer to a back booth away from the juke box. "Okay," he said, when she was seated across from him.

She sighed and looked down so she didn't meet his eyes. Her lashes were dark and thick without mascara. Her hands, toying with the silverware Paddy's put out in the hope that somebody would order more than a drink and fries, were beautiful. She had long, slender fingers like Paige's, and her nails were smooth and shapely, a soft pink even without polish.

"I've been losing sleep over whether or not to talk to you about this, Tuck," Jennifer said quietly. Then she looked up suddenly, her eyes searching his face. "Have you heard the rumor going around school . . . about Mike Lynch?"

Tuck frowned. He wanted to remind her that a southern newcomer without friends didn't hear much of anything, but he only shook his head.

Jennifer took a deep breath and let it out swiftly. "I hate gossip," she said crossly. "I hate all this whispery business. That's why I haven't said anything before but, Tuck, there's an absolutely awful story going around that involves both your sisters. I think you ought to know what everybody is saying, even if there isn't a word of truth in it."

"My sisters?" he asked, strangely relieved. If this was another fight between Paige and Katie, it was bad all right, but it wasn't as terminal as something being wrong between himself and Jennifer.

Jennifer caught one of those quick breaths again and looked at him pleadingly. "Now mind you, Tuck, this is *all* gossip, nothing more."

He nodded. "Go on."

Jennifer traced a pattern on the tablecloth with the tine of a fork as she talked slowly and carefully. "They are saying that Mike Lynch is not making his grades. The only way he is staying on the swim team is because somebody is keeping his grades up *for* him. He does nothing in daily work but is getting by on written work, papers he hands in, and tests. Everyone seems convinced that Katie Guthrie is the one who's doing the cheating for him."

"Not possible!" Tuck said, his voice louder than he meant it to be.

Jennifer put her hand over his and held it tight. "Hush!" she said. "You want everybody in here listening to us?"

He caught her hand tight and dropped his voice. "But it's not possible, Jennifer. Katie's too good a sport, she's a real stickler for stuff like that. The last thing in the world she'd do was help a cheater."

"I'm not arguing with you, Tuck. I'm simply

telling you what everybody is saying. I mean everybody!"

"I'm sorry," Tuck told her. "But you said sisters, plural. How does Paige figure in this?"

Jennifer sighed. "They also say that Paige Whitman is investigating it for the paper, and there's going to be a big article to expose the whole thing."

Tuck sat very still for a minute. Sick. It was just sick the way those girls hated each other. But Katie he was sure of. Paige? Well, she had taken a couple of mean hits at Katie already, why shouldn't she go for this one?"

"Thanks, Jennifer," Tuck said quietly. "Who did you hear this from?"

"Everybody is talking about it. It happened that Jayne Singleton came out and hit me with it first, but I've heard it a dozen times since."

"I don't know Jayne Singleton," Tuck said sullenly. "Why is she blabbing?"

Jennifer smiled and tightened her hand on his. "Nothing personal I'm sure. Jayne Singleton has always been the queen of the whisperers. If there's dirt, she knows all and tells it."

"What do *you* think about all this, Jennifer?" Tuck asked.

"I think it's awful, I said that."

"No, I mean how much truth do you think there could be in it?"

Jennifer looked suddenly uncomfortable. "Oh, Tuck, who knows? Katie is Mike's best friend, and after that faltering start early in the year, she's been a very good student. She's all loyalty to that team. As for Paige . . . I've heard from friends that

41

she's been quietly probing about Mike's performance in his classes. What *can* I think?"

"That it's rotten, just the way I do," Tuck told her. "But I do appreciate your telling me."

"But what can you do?"

"I'll think of something," he assured her. "Let's talk about something that won't spoil our appetites, okay?"

Jennifer made a little face. "I'd love to, Tuck, but I really have to fly."

He glanced at the green leprechaun clock above Paddy's door. Underneath his silly grin, the leprechaun's arms pointed to ten minutes to five. How could it be that late already?

"I'll drive you home," he suggested.

She flushed but met his eyes straight on. "I promised Ed I'd meet him after practice."

Tuck looked at her steadily and held tight to the hand she had tried to pull away. "Eventually you're going to have to choose between us, Jennifer. How about today?"

"You're wrong, Tuck," she said gently. "I don't have to choose anyone. Going with one guy is really stupid with years of school still ahead of me."

"You only went out with Ed before I came along," Tuck reminded her.

She shook her head. "It wasn't like that. I didn't only go with Ed. I just didn't date anyone else."

"Great," he groaned. "Word games."

"I like you. You know how much I like you," Jennifer said.

"Then drop Ed Thomas," Tuck answered swiftly.

42

"He depends on me," Jennifer said, rising. "We've been friends a long time." She stood very still. "Tuck, don't try to push me. It won't work and could only mess up what we've got."

Tuck placed his hand on the small of her back and he guided her toward the door. He could smell her hair, not like perfume but more outdoorsy, like sunshine and spice. "You mean a guy could get penalized for just hoping?"

She laughed softly. "I'd probably hate it if you didn't."

After walking Jennifer back to school, Tuck got into the car. He started the motor, then sat there a long time without backing out. Rumors. Gossip. Like Jennifer, he couldn't stomach these whispering campaigns. If it was time for Ed to be through football practice, then the newspaper office would be shutting down pretty soon, too. Paige was the one to talk to, and he was the one to do it.

He moved the car through the nearly empty lot. After parking it where he could keep an eye on the exits from the building, he tried to concentrate on his history assignment.

Tuck almost beeped the horn when Paige appeared at the door. He hesitated because she wasn't alone. She glanced up at Ben Collins who was holding the door for her, and Tuck was struck by the sadness in her face.

What a strange kid his stepsister was. In spite of all the problems she had made in the family, he had to admit that Paige Whitman was a class act. She was walking slowly beside Ben Collins who was talking to her swiftly and apparently angrily. But Paige's slender back was straight as she listened, her graceful head held high. Her profile as she turned to Ben would have made a great shot — perfect, delicate features accented by the dark hair the wind fanned around her face. As Tuck watched, Ben looked down at her and took her by the shoulders. Paige buried her head against his chest and Ben's arms tightened around her for just a moment. Then Paige was standing alone as Ben waved back at her from his speeding moped.

Instead of honking, Tuck stepped out of the car. "Hey, Paige," he called. "Want a lift home?"

She gave him a startled look like an animal tempted to run. But maybe she was just embarrassed that he had watched that scene with Ben.

She got control quickly and walked toward him. "Why not?" she asked lightly. "What are you doing hanging around here this late?"

He almost told her he had been with Jennifer but stopped himself in time. He didn't want her to guess where he had heard the rumor. "Waiting for you."

Paige's eyes were wary. "What for?"

Tuck forced a grin and drove out of the lot. "To carry you home, as we southerners always say."

Paige laughed softly, then fell silent.

"And to ask you something," he added after a minute. "What's this I hear about your knocking yourself out to get some dirt on Katie?"

He felt her tense in the seat beside him. "I asked you a question," he said after a minute.

"No you didn't," Paige said coldly. "You accused me of something rotten."

"I'm asking now," Tuck said. "Is it true that you're digging into this crazy rumor that Katie is helping Mike Lynch cheat to stay on the team?"

"Tuck, I don't want to talk about that."

"Is that what Ben Collins was barking at you about?" he asked angrily.

"Either stop the car and let me out, or quit shouting at me," Paige said in a firm, warning tone.

Tuck looked at her haughty profile and rammed his foot down on the gas pedal, wanting to reach over and shake her. So what Jennifer had heard *was* straight. He knew in his heart that Katie wasn't doing what she was accused of. But he felt equally sure from Paige's attitude that she was out to pin something on Katie.

Tuck held his tongue until the car was parked in the garage. As Paige opened her door, he couldn't stand it any more. "Aren't you ever going to learn?" he yelled at her.

She didn't indicate she had even heard him but just walked away without looking back.

CHAPTER 5

Paige, for the first time since about the third grade, was tempted to pretend she was sick in order to stay home from school. Nobody could prove she didn't have a sore throat and, given her attendance record, nobody would challenge her. After listening to Ben rant at her for ten minutes to get on the ball, to get the job done, Tuck's accusations were too much. Tuck would never know . . . nobody would ever know . . . how desperately she was fighting to keep the story out of print.

But keeping it out of print apparently wasn't enough. Tuck still didn't have any friends at school except Jennifer Bailey. If the gossip had reached Tuck, it was *really* everywhere.

But even if she stayed home and under the covers of her bed the whole day, the next day would still come.

The minute she walked into the newspaper office she knew she was in trouble. She felt suddenly invisible. Laurie was working at the back of the room on a file. She didn't even turn to greet Paige with her usual wide grin. Carrie wasn't around, but when Paige glanced at Jim Gordon, she saw a bright flush of red rise in his face as he went on typing loudly, as if to drown out her entrance.

Ben was standing by the window, impatiently snapping the cord of the blind and glaring outside at nothing. The minute Paige was inside, Ben whirled, crossed the room, and locked the door behind Paige. He stood with his back against it, looking at them. "Okay," he said furiously. "It's stop the nonsense time."

Paige stood frozen by the coat rack. He couldn't! Ben couldn't possibly mean to criticize her in front of everybody, just because she hadn't done what he wanted.

"Okay, Gordon," Ben snapped. "Tell Whitman what you told me."

Jim jerked his chin up as if his collar were too tight and turned red again. As he spoke, he stared down at his suddenly silenced typewriter. "Well," he began. "One of the guys was talking in the john. Not to me. I was just inside the door, and he hadn't heard me come in. Actually he was laughing."

"Just the facts, Jim," Ben said impatiently.

"He was laughing about how Mike Lynch was pulling the wool over everybody's eyes and holding his slot on the team without ever cracking a book." Jim paused.

"Go on," Ben ordered him. Somebody rattled at the door, but Ben pulled up the shade, motioned the person outside to come back later, and turned back to Jim.

"The other guy said that was a nice trick if you could pull it off." Jim swallowed hard and looked pleadingly at Paige, as if begging her to realize this wasn't his idea. "And the first guy laughed even harder. He said Katie Guthrie was keeping Mike on the team, and she was a nice trick in *anybody's* book."

Ben's eyes, their hazel color gilded by the light, looked steadily at Paige. "Have you heard this, too?" he asked. "Is this why you keep stalling me? Walking around here like the living dead?"

Paige, knowing her voice wasn't going to work, just nodded.

Ben crossed the room in swift, hard strides to stand next to Paige. "What's wrong with your head, Whitman? A story is a story. If the principal of this school was feeding tests and papers to Mike Lynch, I would print it on the first page. Don't you understand? A newspaper is no respecter of persons."

Paige, feeling battered by his loud voice, the hardness of his face against her, flared with anger. "Nothing's wrong with my head . . ." she began.

"Then why are you stalling? If it's that stepsister of yours who's doing the cheating, let's get her, along with Mike Lynch, up on the front page."

"But Ben — " Paige began, only to have him start again.

"Shut up and listen to me!" Paige shouted angrily. At Ben's instant look of surprise, she swallowed hard and lowered her voice. "I haven't any proof against Katie or anyone else. There isn't any evidence. There's only hearsay. But all the information I have gathered *indicates* that Mike Lynch is being carried. Do you really want to accuse an attorney's stepdaughter of an offense that will get her kicked out of school without a shred of evidence to back up your story?"

Ben stared at her, speechless.

"She's right," Laurie said, speaking up for the first time. "She's absolutely right, Ben, and you know it. That's the quickest way I know of to put this paper out of business for good."

"You could have told me what you'd heard," Ben said, his tone a little sullen. Paige wanted to grin. That was the closest she was going to get to an apology, but his expression made her wish there were just the two of them there so she could lean into the warmth of his arms as she had the night before.

"What?" she asked brightly. "And get my head taken off?"

Jim and Laurie both laughed. Ben shrugged. "Point taken. But listen, I meant it when I said whoever is doing this *has* to be caught. I put only Paige on this story because I wanted as few people as possible to know about it. It's out anyway. Now we're all officially on the story. Play it cool but listen. Whoever the cheater is, he or she is going to make a slip. Be there."

Tuck had watched Paige walk out of the garage fully intending to go straight to Katie with the story Jennifer had told him. He didn't catch Katie before dinner and afterward lacked the guts to do it.

The evening meal had been tense enough to give a goat an ulcer.

Paige had sat silent, looking pale and bloodless. Bill Whitman, always conscious of Paige's mood, had glared at her silently all through the meal. Virginia Mae had turned on her nervous social chatter, only relieved by the usual laughter and giggle of the younger girls, who were obviously trying to ignore what was going on.

Tuck himself was glad to escape upstairs to the dubious pleasures of homework. "Tomorrow is soon enough anyway," he kidded himself, dreading Katie's reaction to what he had to tell her.

He missed Katie before dinner the next night but followed her upstairs and asked her to come into his room.

"Why?" she asked, smiling expectantly as if he had some surprise for her.

"I want to talk to you a minute," he told her.

"We can talk here," she said. "What's up?"

"I can't do it out here," Tuck said crossly. "Come on."

"Does it *have* to be right now, Tuck?" Katie asked, her expression curious but reluctant. "Jake's due any minute. It's our first time together in *ages*."

Tuck grinned. Sure Katie, whole generations of dinosaurs have fallen to dust since you and Jake went out last week. "It's important," he told her. "Come on."

Katie's curiosity won out. Tuck shut the door and waited while she sank down on his bed.

"Well?" she said, her eyes narrowing as she sensed his own nervousness. "I'm here. Talk."

"Katie," Tuck said, trying to keep his voice calm. "Now just listen to me and don't blow up. There's a story all over school, and I mean *all* over school. The word is that Mike Lynch is being kept on the swim team by cheating."

"That's not true," Katie said, jumping to her feet.

Tuck put his hand on her shoulder and pushed her back down. "Keep your voice down and listen to me."

"Mike is not a cheater," she whispered hotly.

"I didn't say he was. I said that story is all over school. And that's not the worst of it. They're also saying that *you're* the one who's helping him so he can swim."

Katie caught a deep breath, and her brilliant blue eyes narrowed. "Tucker Guthrie. That is the *ugliest* thing I have ever heard in my life. Mike's not a cheater. But even if he were, that wouldn't make me one, too. I wouldn't know how to go about it, if I were filthy enough to do it." She paused and stared at him. "Paige," she said quickly. "Nobody in the whole world would start a rumor like that against Mike and me except Paige Whitman." Suddenly Katie's expressive eyes were shining with tears.

"Katie," Tuck said. "Come on, don't bawl. . . ."

"Bawl!" she whispered fiercely. "Who's going to bawl?" She tugged a tissue from her pocket and wiped her eyes. "That Paige Whitman. She started

51

this. She's bad, Tuck, bad, evil, malicious, horrible. I know it, Tuck, Paige started this, and she'll be sorrier than she's ever been in her life before it's over." Katie fled past him and out of the room, slamming the door behind her.

Tuck breathed out slowly, half expecting an explosion from the room down the hall that Katie shared with Paige. Nothing. All that probably meant was that Paige wasn't there. It was just as well. Katie would need some time to get herself under control to handle this one.

Tuck opened his book and stared at it without seeing the print. After a few moments, he heard the doorbell ring downstairs and his mother calling Katie.

Katie didn't dance down the stairs as she usually did when she was going to meet Jake. Her steps were quick, but they were angry steps, firm and hard against the floor.

Poor Katie. But poor Jake, too. He didn't envy Jake his evening with Katie Summer Guthrie on the warpath.

CHAPTER 6

Jake, standing in the hall, grinned up at Katie as she came down the stairs. He caught her hand and squeezed it hard. "Smashing as always," he said approvingly. "I've looked forward to this all day."

Katie only smiled. She had looked forward to seeing *him* all day, too, but now she wasn't sure she could deal with the evening ahead. Tuck's words had left her bubbling with so much anger and resentment that she was going to have trouble thinking about anything else. As she slid into her coat Jake caught her in a quick hug. Her breath came short. If he would just never let go! How safe it felt to have Jake's arms tight around her like that.

But of course he let go. Within minutes they were in his car. He looked over at her soberly. "We were invited out tonight, but I turned the invitation down."

"Invited out? Where?" she asked, dragging her mind back from her problem.

"Gary was released from the hospital today," Jake explained. "He and Midge wanted us to come watch a movie with them on Gary's VCR."

"And you didn't want to?" Katie asked.

Jake shook his head. "Gary rented some picture I've seen a dozen times, and anyway, I want to talk to you about a rumor I heard."

She stared at him. This wasn't possible! He couldn't have heard that awful rumor about her and Mike Lynch, too! But he looked so very serious, almost forbidding, that she felt her heart sink.

"I heard," Jake said ominously, "that you have been spying on me. That you came secretly and hid somewhere up in the grandstand, watched my team play, and then sneaked away without even a word for the substitute coach."

There was laughter in his voice as he glanced at her.

"Oh that!" Katie said, practically weak with relief. "I didn't *sneak* away. I just had to get back home. And anyway, you were too busy with your players to know who was in the grandstand."

Jake was laughing at her. "Gary told me about your coming. Actually he confessed that he sent Midge to check up on me and the team, and she hauled you along. Aren't they the best? Those girls really have something going for themselves. No wonder Gary gets so excited about them."

She nodded. "They're something all right. And it was a good game."

"If I can just hold them together and keep them

winning until Gary gets back on his feet, I'll think I've done something. Did you notice the blonde girl wearing number seventeen? Her name's Sandy and she's a wonder. I think she could hold her own on a boys' team. And she's fun, too. Good sense of humor."

Katie sat quietly as Jake went on and on about how much fun all the girls were and how hard they worked out to keep up their speed and their shots. "And what team spirit," he said. "Those girls would do anything for each other."

His words echoed in her mind, bringing back a rush of anger. "Do anything for each other." Was that what team spirit was all about, doing *anything* for the other members, even helping them cheat to be on the team? Not in her book it wasn't, and if Paige thought she was going to pin that on Mike or herself, she was just plain wrong!

Katie stirred angrily in her seat. She shouldn't have come out with Jake. She was too mad to settle down and be good company. Not that she had a chance to be anything but a good listener with Jake blabbering on forever about his team. She wished he would just quit talking and drive.

"So what are we going to do?" Katie asked suddenly.

Jake sat in silence for a moment, then she felt him looking over at her. She continued to stare straight ahead.

"Sure, Katie," he said, his tone giving away his annoyance. "Sorry if I bored you stiff. But you know how it is when you're all wrapped up in something new."

"I didn't mean to sound rude," Katie told him. "I guess I just have a lot on my mind."

"Anything you want to talk about?"

She hesitated. She didn't really trust herself to tell him what Tuck had told her. How could she explain it without making it sound as if she were picking on Paige?

She shook her head. "It's too unpleasant to talk about."

"Okay," Jake said. From his tone she knew he was still annoyed by the way she had broken into his conversation. "In answer to your earlier question, I thought we'd catch the movie that's running over by the school. The kids on the team told me it was worth seeing. Sound okay?"

It didn't sound okay. She didn't need to listen to all that stuff about his team and then sit through a movie they picked out. "I can't imagine any movie that is worth seeing tonight," she admitted.

"That bad?" Jake asked, his tone suddenly sympathetic.

Katie nodded. "Like you said, I'm too wrapped up in something new to think about anything else." She looked at him. "Could we just go somewhere and talk?"

He laid his hand on hers. "Paddy's place okay?"

She hesitated, then shook her head. "Maybe some place where there wouldn't be any kids from my school?"

He nodded and drove silently to a pizza restaurant named Figlio's that she had never even seen before. By the time they were sitting at a tiny round table under a window filled with blooming plants, she realized she was trembling.

56

Jake ordered, then took both her hands in his and looked over at her. "Okay, Chicken Little! Go on and tell me that the world is coming to an end."

She stared at him. Couldn't he tell she was really having a problem? "Don't make fun of me," Katie said, tempted to pull her hands away. "You know I don't make a big fuss over nothing."

"Katie," he laughed. "Of course you do! I list that in with your other fatal charms. Everything that happens to Katie Summer Guthrie is larger than life. Never a dull moment."

"This *is* larger than life," she said as firmly as she could without barking at him.

"The end of the world?" he asked.

Why did he have to do this? When she felt playful he was moody and dour. Now that she wanted to be serious, he had to carry on like this!

"Okay, Jake," she said hotly. "How would you feel if someone started an ugly rumor that you were a cheater?"

He stared at her, his expression turning serious. "Wait a minute." he said. "Fill in the blanks. Who's someone? Cheating at what?"

Katie dropped her eyes. "Never mind the someone. But there's a nasty rumor going around school that Mike Lynch is failing his grades and that I'm keeping him qualified for the swim team."

"Is he pulling in failing grades?" Jake asked.

She shrugged. "How do I know? I don't have classes with him. I'm a sophomore and he's a senior."

"Come on, Katie," Jake scoffed. "If anything

like that is going on, the whole team knows about it."

"I don't know any such thing," she said hotly.

"Maybe you *would* be the last to know," Jake said thoughtfully. "Just like you'd be the first one to be suspected of helping him."

"That's awful," Katie cried. "I don't even know why I'm talking to you, if you're going to be that way about it. Mike's a good sport. I can't believe he's a cheater. But even if he were, why should *I* be blamed for helping him or anybody cheat?"

"Because *you* are the team's other star. In a case like that, they always look for another person with a lot to lose if the team falls behind."

"Then they ought to look for a senior who is trying for an athletic scholarship," Katie said angrily.

"That's fair enough, but Mike doesn't spend his time squiring any seniors around. You set yourself up to be suspected when you hang around with him."

"Hang around with him!" Katie repeated angrily. "We're friends. He gives me rides home. Is that hanging around?"

Jake's eyes were cold on hers. "*Yes!* And if you remember, this isn't the first time we've talked about this."

Katie flushed but said nothing. He was jealous, that was all.

"Have you talked to Lynch about this?" Jake asked.

Katie's eyes flew wide with amazement. "I don't believe you said that. I would be insulting Mike to talk to him about anything as awful as this."

"Even if you're best friends?" Jake asked, in a goading tone. "Who told you . . . an arch enemy?"

She stared at him. "Tuck told me," she finally said, her voice almost a whisper.

Jake shrugged. "I win that point."

"I didn't realize we were keeping score," she said.

He leaned toward her, his eyes level on hers. "Katie, use your head instead of just blowing off. You know Tuck told you for your own good, and that he doesn't believe a word of it any more than I do. He knows you too well, just as I do. If you were as sure of this Mike Lynch being on the level as Tuck is of you, you could talk it over with him."

"*This* Mike Lynch," Katie repeated angrily. "You want to believe the worst of Mike because you don't like him."

"I'm expected to like a guy who's after my girl?" Jake asked. His words caught Katie off-guard. Had he ever called her his girl before? But even as she felt herself warmed by his words, he ruined it. "But if Lynch is flunking out, he's going to get caught in the end. The farther you stay away from him the better."

"I want to go home," Katie said.

Jake rose without a word, laid a tip on the table, and handed her coat to her.

In the darkness of the car, he spoke quietly. "I'm sorry that what I said made you mad, Katie. But where there's smoke, there's fire, and you shouldn't hang around to get burned."

"It was dumb of me to tell you," she said stiffly. "I listened to all that stuff about your precious girls without a word, but the minute I mention Mike Lynch's name you light into me with a lecture."

"You think I said all that just because I'm jealous?" he asked.

"In fact, I do," Katie said, angered by his tone.

"Then you don't know me as well as I thought you did," he said, pulling his car into the curb in front of the house. His tone was patronizing, as if she were not only a child but a very stupid one.

She didn't have to accept that from him or anyone! She jerked the door open and started quickly up the front walk toward the house. He was out of the car and beside her in a few swift steps. He caught her by the shoulders, whirled her around, and kissed her in a fierce, angry way. Surprised, she struggled against him for a moment before returning his kiss and clinging to him.

Then he held her away and looked at her very angrily. "Blast it, Katie! There's no getting through to you, is there? Mike Lynch doesn't mean anything to me. He can live or die for all I care. But I care about you. Stay away from that guy until this rumor dies down."

Katie's mother and Bill Whitman were still out. The house was quiet and dimly lit, with only a table lamp glowing in the living room. Katie went into the kitchen, poured a glass of milk, and sat staring out into the dark backyard.

Mike Lynch couldn't be cheating. He wasn't that sort. She was sure of it, absolutely positive. Anyway, who could be helping him? There were only one or two guys that he went around with, and both of them were on the team, too.

She gasped. Jake had done this to her! Jake had twisted her mind around to where she was actually considering that Mike *could* be cheating. Angrily she rinsed out her glass and set it in the dishwasher. She pushed her blonde hair off her forehead.

Mike wasn't cheating. The whole thing was a lie Paige had made up just to make her miserable. Jake had said the truth would come out. When that happened, it wouldn't be Mike who would be in trouble but Paige herself. In the meantime, Katie simply *had* to talk about it to somebody whose head wasn't all bent by jealousy.

CHAPTER 7

Katie had felt relaxed and comfortable in almost every situation of her life. During the morning after her talk with Tuck, she found out how different and uncomfortable it felt to be self-conscious all the time.

At first she thought she was makings things up and tried to be really honest with herself.

Had she imagined the sudden silence that fell when she entered the women's washroom? Nobody looked at her and nobody spoke. For the space of a minute you could have heard a pin drop. Then one of the juniors, a thin, jittery girl with dark hair and large teeth, giggled nervously. Katie stubbornly combed out her curls, washed her hands, and dried them carefully so they would know they hadn't driven her out. Let them snicker! She had left of her own accord.

Was she imagining that every time she made

eye-contact with anyone in the hall, that other person looked away? Why did she feel that eyes were probing into her back whenever she went from one classroom to another? She counted the minutes until noon when she could see her friends.

Katie raced out of class to be at the cafeteria door when Lisa and Sara arrived. She made it in time only to realize that both of them greeted her with extra warmth, even though their expressions were more sympathetic than welcoming.

"How about lunch?" Katie asked, looking from one to the other.

"Sure," Lisa said, starting in.

Katie shook her head. "I mean how about lunch somewhere else. I'll buy."

They looked at each other again, searchingly. Then Lisa shrugged. "Why not? It's an open campus." She grinned. "Usually we're just too lazy and too poor."

"And we will have to hurry back," Sara added, checking her watch. "Paddy's service is really slow."

"We can get sandwiches and drinks at the deli and eat them there," Katie said. "I really need to talk to you both."

The air in the deli was rich with the mingled scents of pickles and cold meats and fresh coffee. When they took their food to the last small available table, Katie knew for certain that both Sara and Lisa knew what she wanted to talk about. They had already heard the rumor or they would have asked what was up. Also, they were both self-conscious, eating their sandwiches as carefully as if corned beef on rye came with twenty dollar bills between the slices of bread.

"Okay," Katie said. "Let's compare slander."

Lisa looked up with a genuine expression of dismay. "Oh, Katie," she said. "We kept hoping you wouldn't hear."

"The whole story is so ridiculous," Sara added. "We thought it might just die down and go away." She frowned. "Who told you, anyway?"

"My brother," Katie said shortly. "Now tell me what you heard so I can compare notes."

"It's all a dirty, filthy lie and everybody knows it," Lisa said angrily. Then, after a glance at Katie's face, she repeated almost exactly what Tuck had told Katie the night before. The only part she left out was the part about Paige. Lisa ended with a further protest. "Nobody believes it. They can't."

"And my stepsister isn't mentioned in all of this?" Katie asked, suddenly unable even to make herself say Paige's name aloud.

Again they looked at each other before facing her. "Your brother dumped the whole load on you, didn't he?" Sara asked a little bitterly. "The word is that Paige Whitman is going around quietly asking all sorts of questions about Mike Lynch and his classes."

"Does anybody say why?"

"She's supposed to be putting together a big story on cheating athletes," Lisa said. "Honest, Katie, we kept hoping — "

Katie smiled as convincingly as she could. "That's okay. I understand. Is Mike really flunking?" She hated herself the minute the words were out. She would never have asked them if Jake hadn't lectured her so hard the night before.

"That depends on who's talking," Lisa told her. "Nobody claims he's any scholar, but only the people who can't stand him say he's getting through on somebody else's work. Are you sure you don't know? We sort of figured you knew and didn't want to tell anyone."

"I don't even believe Mike is cheating," Katie told her. "But if somebody's helping him, it's sure not me."

Lisa looked at Sara and laughed. "We talked that over, too," she told Katie. "We decided it was one thing to drag your grades back up, the way you did early in the year, and quite another to drag a lumpish senior through courses you'd never had. Sorry about that, kid, we just didn't think you had it in you."

Katie grinned and shoved her half eaten sandwich away. "Thanks, team!" she said.

"What do *you* think is going on?" Lisa asked.

Katie couldn't keep the anger from her voice. "I think Mike's clean, and I know I am. I think that my ever-conniving stepsister is out to knock me off that team no matter how many lies she has to tell to do it."

"They can't print a word until they have proof," Sara reminded her.

"Does that stop any of the gossip?"

Lisa frowned thoughtfully, took her paper plate, and tossed it into the trash basket on the first try. "Got any ideas? We couldn't come up with any."

"If I could just find out who *started* it!" Katie wailed.

"Paige," Sara said quickly. "Her name has been mentioned every time I've been told about it. Quote, Did you hear about Paige Whitman gathering evidence that Katie Gathrie is keeping Mike Lynch on the team by helping him with his grades, question mark, end quote."

Katie breathed deeply, fighting an urge to scream with fury. "I could just kill that monster girl," she said softly.

Lisa tugged on her coat. "If she doesn't get you first. Let's get out of here. It's almost time for the bell. And believe me, Katie, if we hear any more, we'll let you know."

At the end of the school day, Katie took a different route to the swimming pool. She deliberately chose the hall where Paige and Judy had lockers. She waited a few feet away as they approached.

Judy saw her first and nudged Paige. Paige's face grew pale, and she turned to walk the other way as fast as she could. Katie ran after her and caught her by the arm.

"Keep your hands off me," Paige whispered fiercely.

"I want to talk to you."

"I don't want to talk to *you*," Paige said, starting off again. A bunch of passing kids slowed down to watch.

"Don't fool yourself that I won't make a scene if that's what you want," Katie warned her. "I just want to talk to you."

66

Paige pretended to be scornful, but Katie saw the fear in her eyes. "That's your style all right, Katie Summer Guthrie. We *all* know how much you like to be center stage. Make two scenes if you have time. I don't have to talk to you now or any time away from that house."

At that, Paige turned and walked away rapidly. A girl Katie didn't know laughed loudly from the center of the watching group. She spoke to Katie in an exaggerated southern drawl. "Whatcha doing, honey? Giving our star reporter some help with her grades?"

Katie turned and stared at her. Then, realizing that her eyes were glistening with tears of rage and frustration, she wheeled and went rapidly toward the gym.

Bill Whitman had to choose that night to talk about the new restaurant that had opened downtown. "It's really an interesting place," he told Virginia Mae as Paige and Katie sat silently, not meeting each other's eyes. "It's basically Italian with all the pasta made right there. The menu features specialties from all the different regions of Italy. They have dishes I've never heard of. Both you girls like pasta, don't you?"

"I like canned spaghetti," Megan piped up. "Right out of the can cold."

When Mary Emily collapsed in an imitation choking fit, Tuck laughed. "Don't let her run you down, Megan. She likes the mix that comes in a box."

By the time the table settled down again, Bill's question had been lost in the shuffle. But Katie's decision had been made. There was no way that she was going to sit down and pretend to get along with Paige Whitman with everything that was going on.

When the rest of the family had left and the table was cleared, Katie followed her mother into the study. Virginia Mae looked around with a curious expression as Katie closed the door behind them. Katie's hand on the doorknob was clammy with fear. There had been too many angry words between her and her mother since the marriage. But this time her mother had to listen. Paige wouldn't talk to her. She didn't dare bring it up to Mike. Her mother simply *had* to listen and get out of this horrible Saturday date Bill Whitman was planning.

"What's up, Katie?" Virginia Mae asked, taking her seat on the piano bench.

"I need to talk to you," Katie said breathlessly.

Virginia Mae's smile held a touch of mischief. "Clothes again?"

As Katie shook her head, Bill Whitman rapped softly on the door. "Men admitted?" he asked.

Before her mother could reply, Katie spoke swiftly. "Mom, I *really* need to talk to you, alone. Just a little while."

Virginia Mae studied Katie silently, then rose, and went to the door. "I'm sorry, Bill. Katie and I are having a little mother-daughter heart-to-heart. We won't be long. All right?"

Katie heard his soft chuckle. "Go to it. I have a brief I should read through anyway."

Virginia Mae went to the sofa and drew Katie

down beside her. "Now, what do you want to talk about?" she asked gently.

"I have a problem," Katie said, trying very hard not to choke up. The gentleness in her mother's voice, just like the old days, flooded her with yearning.

"Just so you aren't bringing me a problem about Paige," her mother said firmly. "You know I won't hear any of that."

Katie sighed and groped for words. Why had she thought she would get any help here? The loneliness of her predicament swept over her.

"My problem is that I can't have lunch with Bill on Saturday," she told her mother quietly.

"But Katie," her mother cried. "You promised him. He set this date up almost two weeks ago."

"I know it," Katie said. "But I really can't do it. And I'm sorry."

"This isn't socially responsible behavior, Katie." Her mother's tone turned stern. "We don't accept invitations and then cancel at the last minute without reason."

"I have a reason, but you've already told me I can't mention it."

Virginia sighed and rose. "Oh, Katie, please don't tell me that you and Paige are into another one of your ridiculous childish battles."

"I won't," Katie said. "I'm simply telling you that I absolutely cannot go to that lunch Saturday, and I'm asking you to tell Bill."

"Katie," her mother said, perching beside her again. "How can you ask me to tell my husband, who loves you dearly, that you can't stand to share a single public meal alone with him and his daughter? Isn't that a little much to ask me to do?"

"It isn't any worse than making me go under the circumstances."

Virginia Mae looked at her a long time, sighed, then took her hands. "All right, Katie. Tell me these circumstances. Be as objective as you possibly can and remember that I won't listen to any slander about Paige. Why can't you go?"

Suddenly Katie fought tears. She wiped her eyes with the backs of her hands and forced the words out carefully. "There's a rumor all over school that the star of the swimming team is cheating to make grades to stay on the team."

"Katie," her mother cried, but Katie shook her head.

"Please let me finish," she begged. "It's supposed to be Mike Lynch. You know Mike. The story goes that *I* am the person helping him cheat."

"That's awful!" her mother said, genuinely shocked. "You'd never do a thing like that. They should know that." She paused. "Mike doesn't seem the sort either. Oh, Katie, this is just terrible." Then she frowned. "But what has this to do with your having lunch with Paige and Bill?"

Katie blew out her breath slowly and tightened her arms against her sides. "Everybody says that Paige is at the bottom of the gossip. She started it by going around asking questions of all Mike's classmates. I tried to ask her about it, but she won't talk to me."

"How long has this been going on?" Virginia Mae asked.

"I don't know," Katie admitted. "All my friends had heard it, but they didn't tell me. I only heard it this week."

"Your friends didn't tell you?" Virginia Mae asked.

Katie shook her head.

"Then who did?"

Katie hesitated. She had been tempted at the first to tell her mother to ask Tuck, but that didn't seem very sporting. It might look to her mother as if she and Tuck were ganging up on Paige, when it wasn't that way at all.

"Katie," her mother prodded her. "Who told you?"

"Tuck," Katie said softly. "Ask him if you want to. He thought I ought to know. I'm glad he did, but, oh, Mom. . ." The tears came without warning as Virginia Mae took her into her arms. Virginia Mae rocked her gently a minute, until Katie caught her breath and got herself under control.

Virginia Mae wiped at Katie's eyes with a handkerchief that smelled of her wonderful floral scent. Then she lifted a moist blonde curl back from Katie's forehead.

"I don't think I need to talk to Tuck," she said quietly. "But I *will* talk to Bill. Don't worry about it any more."

Katie snuggled against her mother, but in spite of the warmth of Virginia Mae's arms, Katie only felt despair.

CHAPTER 8

The evening began to become strange as Paige went through the hall to go upstairs after dinner. Katie and Virginia Mae went into the study together which was a little unusual. Paige was still on the stairs when she saw her father rap at the closed study door and go inside. Although he came back out immediately, she heard his parting remark, "Go to it. I have a brief I should read through anyway."

"Go to it!" That meant that Katie and Virginia Mae were going to have another of their "talks," which usually ended with Katie losing her temper and stamping off. Paige pressed herself against the wall so her father wouldn't notice her and think she was eavesdropping. He didn't glance up as he took his briefcase from the hall closet and crossed into the living room. She breathed out with relief when he disappeared into the room without glancing up. Then a prickle of real terror crawled along her spine. She felt sure that Katie was going to tell her mother about the scene Katie had made at school and how Paige had rebuffed her attempts to talk.

Even Judy had been upset at Paige, upset enough to walk away mad.

"Why didn't you talk to her?" Judy asked with amazement as Katie walked swiftly toward the gym. "Why make a big deal of it?"

"She hasn't anything to say I want to hear," Paige said, annoyed at Judy's attitude. "And I sure don't have anything I want to say to *her*."

Judy breathed out sharply with disgust. "Honestly, Paige, I don't get you sometimes. *I* know what she wanted to talk to you about, and you do, too! She's finally heard that crazy rumor that everybody in school is whispering, about her and Mike Lynch . . . and you. All you had to do was *tell* her it was just hoked-up gossip."

"I don't want to talk about it," Paige said angrily.

Judy had stood very still, staring at her. "It *is* only rumor, isn't it, Paige?"

"I said — " Paige began, only to have Judy interrupt her.

"I heard what you said. I also know you, Paige Whitman. You are a world class bad liar. That's the same as saying that it *isn't* a rumor. You really *are* going around trying to pin something on Katie. That's mean, Paige, just plain ugly and mean."

At that Judy had turned and walked away, her neck stiff. "Wait," Paige called after her desperately. "Let me explain."

Judy turned at her words and stared at her as if she barely knew Paige and didn't like what she *did* know. "You don't want to talk about it. Remember?" Judy asked acidly, and left.

Paige stood inside the doorway of her bedroom, shivering. The room itself was dark, but through the window came a faint glow from the lights that lined the paths in the park across the street. Katie's cat startled her by rising from a hump of covers on Paige's bed. Binker stretched and meowed at Paige in a cordial way. Then she leaped to the floor, crossed the room, and began rubbing her warm body against Paige's leg. Paige knelt and petted the cat absentmindedly. Binker's soft back rose to her hand and the cat purred contentedly.

The contrast between the cat's placid rumble and the storm of fear and resentment that boiled inside Paige's mind was too great. "Oh, go away," she said, shoving the cat aside. "Just go away and leave me alone."

Turning on her bed lamp, Paige pulled up her covers, lay on her stomach, and began to study, only to find her mind running out of control.

She didn't look up when Katie came in, deliberately whistling softly. Katie changed her clothes, and then went out again. Her stepsister's whistle scared Paige. So Virginia Mae had listened to her. Paige felt a painful stiffness pull at the back of her neck, guessing what would happen next. Virginia Mae would go right to her husband with Katie's story. Paige groaned to herself, this must not lead to another one of those awful battles with her dad. If she hadn't been afraid that Katie would come in and see her, she would have just put her head down and cried.

Then the sound of splashing water came from the bathroom. Over it, Paige could hear Katie humming to herself. Desperate to get away before Katie came back, smelling of bath powder and body lotion and whatever else she smeared on herself when she bathed, Paige gathered up her books and went downstairs, hoping to get into the playroom to study without anyone seeing her.

Paige was near the bottom of the stairs when she heard her father talking. She couldn't hear his words, only the deep rumble of his voice. Whatever he said must have made Virginia Mae mad because she spoke hotly, sounding very much like an older Katie in the swift drawling anger of her tone.

"Very well, Bill," Virginia Mae said. Paige heard a chair scrape as if her stepmother had risen swiftly. "I won't argue with you. You obviously aren't going to listen to me anyway. Ask Paige. *If* you dare, ask Paige for yourself."

Paige fled down the hall, her heart thundering. She had never heard Virginia Mae speak to her husband in a tone like that. And her father's words, as Paige fled, were as harsh with anger as they had been when he had lectured Paige. "I'm glad you suggested that," he said furiously. "Because that's *exactly* what I intend to do."

Paige was barely inside the playroom with the door closed when she heard Virginia Mae cross the hall and run up the stairs. Paige waited, her heart thundering, feeling the moments crawl by before her father came looking for her.

Since he didn't know she was in the playroom, he called for her at the bottom of the stairs. "Paige?"

She opened the door and answered, grateful that for once her voice didn't crack in an emergency.

"Come in the study, Paige," he said. His tone was quiet and a little sad but not angry at all. "I need to talk something over with you."

When Paige followed him into the study, he closed the door behind her. He waited until she was seated, then perched on the piano bench, looking at her. "Our household is into heart-to-heart talks tonight," he said in a mocking tone that gave away his concern. "I think it's time we had one of our own."

Paige tightened her hands together and waited.

"I want you to tell me what is going on at school between you and Katie," he said.

Paige stared at a spot a little to the right of his shoulder, trying to decide what to do. What did he know? Was this about the scene today or the whole mess about Mike Lynch? It would help if she knew what Katie had told her mother.

"Well?" he prodded, still gently. "Something is clearly happening. You've been walking around here like a zombie for days, and now Katie comes to her mother with a story that's very hard for me to swallow."

The painful conflict she had been fighting flooded Paige with a sense of exhaustion. She didn't care what Katie had told her mother or what her father and Virginia Mae had fought about. She had needed to tell somebody what she was going through, and he was offering her this chance.

"May I tell it from the first?" she asked meekly.

He nodded, his hands loose in his lap. "Any way that's the best."

"It started with a rumor at a basketball game," she told him, describing the argument Ben had gotten into. "I tried every way I knew to get Ben to assign somebody else to the story. I didn't want to deal with it because Katie was on the team and all." He nodded understanding as she went on. "I couldn't stand to let Ben down so I started asking questions, really carefully I thought. I didn't know anything about Mike Lynch or whether he was cheating. It was just a story Ben asked me to do, and I made myself do it."

She sighed and stopped, feeling as if she'd run out of steam.

"And has Mike been cheating?" he asked.

"He doesn't ever do anything in class, but his tests and papers are good."

"That's suspicious. But I still don't see how Katie is involved."

"I don't *know* that she is," Paige told him. "Other people say that. The story got back to Ben, and he jumped all over me. He said if Katie was helping Mike cheat, they both had to be exposed, no matter whose sister she was."

"Why do people say Katie is the one doing this?" he asked.

Paige shrugged. "I think it's what you'd call circumstantial. She and Mike are really good

77

friends and people see them together a lot. Katie's stayed on honors track since that first probation. You never see Mike with many other people." Paige shrugged. "And they are the big stars on that team, both really gung-ho to win the conference."

"Do *you* think Katie could be helping Mike cheat?"

Paige suddenly felt cold. She had never said this aloud to a human being. She struggled for breath and couldn't find it. She nodded and then felt her tears begin. "She's the only person *anybody* mentions. Ben is on me every day to clear this up, but I can't accuse her or anybody without facts. I really don't know what to do."

"Have you tried to talk to Katie about it?"

She shook her head. "She stopped me at school today with people walking all around. I just couldn't deal with it there and wouldn't talk to her. Didn't Virginia Mae tell you that?"

He shook his head. "She came to tell me that Katie felt she couldn't go to lunch with us because of a problem between the two of you."

"Virginia Mae didn't say anything about this Mike Lynch business?"

"Only after I pressed her. I told her that unless Katie was guilty of this charge she should be able to face us over lunch no matter what." He shrugged. "I'm afraid I made her pretty angry." He grinned with no humor in his face. "Maybe I need to sleep on the couch tonight?"

Paige ached for the hurt in his face. "Oh, Dad, I'm so sorry. I tried to stay out of this. I've hated every minute of it. I just don't know what to do."

Bill Whitman rose, pulled Paige to her feet, and put his arms around her. "Poor Paige. The hardest thing in the world is to face truths you don't want to accept. I'm sorry you got caught in this, Paige, but the truth *has* to come out in the end."

He was walking her toward the door. She clung to him. "But what am I going to do?"

"Your job," he said quietly. "I'm with Ben on that. The truth is no respecter of persons." His choice of words jolted her. Ben had said almost the same thing about the newspaper.

Paige buried her head in her father's chest, trying to hold back her tears. "But I'm so miserable," she whispered. "And so tired."

He held her close a minute, then looked down into her face. "Try to put this out of your mind and get some sleep, honey," he said gently.

"But, Dad," Paige protested. "It's so hard."

"It's *always* hard when you're caught between loyalties," he said quietly. "Believe me. I know."

When Katie returned to the room to find Paige gone, she was only half glad. While she had no intention of saying anything to Paige, she knew it would drive her stepsister crazy just to have Katie act happy. Paige had seen Katie and her mother go into the study together. Paige probably thought Katie was telling Virginia Mae about that stupid scene at school. Never mind what she thought. Just let Paige worry about what was going to happen.

And Katie's happy feeling wasn't totally put on. That had been the first good talk with her mother in a long long time, almost since she and

Bill Whitman had married. Her mother had really *listened*, and really cared. And her mother never broke promises. She wouldn't have said she would talk to Bill about that ridiculous Saturday lunch unless she meant to do it.

Katie stood at the window, brushing her hair and staring down into the park. Now what would happen? Once Paige's father found out what Paige was up to, he would put a stop to it.

She paused. Her arm holding the brush went limp as she felt her happiness drain away. What good was it going to do for Paige's father to blow up and lay the law down to Paige again? That wouldn't stop the rumors at school. It wouldn't keep people from looking at her as if she had suddenly broken out in hives.

Katie sighed, shoved Binker off her pillow, and slid into bed. "Win a little battle and lose a big war," she told the cat miserably. "I get out of having to have lunch with Paige, but there isn't any way I'm ever going to get my good name back."

As she spoke, she heard someone come up the stairs. The footsteps sounded like her mother's, only quicker and angrier than Virginia Mae ever walked. Then they stopped and a door slammed hard.

Katie frowned a moment, stepped into the hall, and stood very still. Light suddenly streamed from under Virginia Mae's door as a lamp was turned on inside. It *had* been her mother. Still staring thoughtfully, she heard voices in the hall below, Bill Whitman calling Paige out of that little hole of a playroom where she went and pretended to study. "Come in the study, Paige," he said quietly. "I need to talk something over with you."

This was what Katie had wanted, for Paige's father to know what Paige was up to, for Paige to be in trouble again.

But her stepfather's voice didn't sound angry, hurt maybe, and thoughtful, but not angry. And he hadn't said he wanted to "talk to her." Talking something over was different. The door to the study closed, plunging the downstairs hall in darkness.

Katie shivered. Her mother had listened to her and believed her. Her mother was taking her part. But from the way Virginia Mae had run upstairs and slammed into her room, Katie knew she and Bill had fought about it. They had never fought before and the idea was scary.

What if Paige's father did the same thing? What if he took Paige's part against Katie and was as mad as her mother acted? Paige would have to lie to him to make him think she was in the right, but Paige wouldn't stop at lying.

Katie hesitated a moment, then walked down the hall, and tapped softly on Tuck's door. "Yes?" he asked in a tone that clearly expressed his resentment at being bothered.

"I want to talk to you," she whispered.

"I'm studying," he said.

"Let me in," Katie insisted, trying the door handle and finding it locked.

He turned the key and stood in the open door,

glaring down at her. "Make it fast," he told her.

She slid past him and motioned him to close the door.

Tuck sighed and obeyed. "You're wasting my time," he grumbled. "I told you everything I know about that Mike Lynch business."

She laid a finger on her lips to caution him to silence. "This isn't about that," she whispered. "Something awful is happening with Mom and Bill."

Tuck tightened his lips and shook his head. "Don't come in here sounding like a soap opera, Katie," he said crossly. "I'm tired of your dramatics and Paige's surliness. Mom and Bill are the only human beings in this place who have their act together."

"They had a fight," Katie said sullenly.

"So, they're human," he said.

"But you still don't understand," Katie insisted. "I told Mom what Paige is doing to me, that Mike Lynch business. She really listened and promised to talk to Bill."

Tuck fell silent and studied her face a moment. "What can Bill do about it?" he asked.

Katie shook her head. "Not believe her, that's what. After they talked, Mom ran off up here and slammed her door as if they'd had a fight about it."

"As if," he echoed. "You're jumping to conclusions and they are *bad* ones. Listen to me, Katie Summer, the worst thing that can happen to any of us is for those two to start taking sides against the other one's kids. Don't even *think* that. You might make it happen."

"It's already happened," Katie whispered stubbornly.

Tuck opened the door and nudged her out into the hall. "Go to bed and sleep off your bad dreams." As he spoke, Bill's voice came quietly up the stairs.

"Try to put this out of your mind and get some sleep, honey," he said gently.

"But, Dad," Paige protested. "It's so hard."

"It's always hard when you're caught between loyalties," he said quietly. "Believe me. I know."

When Katie looked up at Tuck, he whistled silently and shook his head, before motioning Katie on toward her room.

CHAPTER 9

Katie, wearing a daffodil yellow sweater with a blue scarf that matched her eyes, swung her book bag and hummed to herself as she ran up the front steps of school. She almost charged into Lisa Conrad who was waiting just inside the front door. Lisa laughed and spoke to Sara at her side, "Well, I guess this was a wasted drill!"

"What drill?" Katie asked, stopping still before falling into step with her friends.

Lisa grinned at her. "Sara and I decided to get here early and cheer you up before you faced another day being ground up in the gossip mill. But look at you! If you were any cheerier, you'd look like a vitamin commercial."

"It's a soap opera," Katie corrected her. "At least that's what my brother called it last night."

"But things *must* be looking up," Sara said. "Else how could you be so perky?"

"I'm auditioning a new role," Katie told her,

nodding solemnly. "I decided on it this morning during breakfast. If we *must* have a soap opera, I get to pick my part. We can't *all* be heavies, you know. Somebody has to play young, innocent, and lighthearted."

"Breakfast?" Sara asked. "Are you serious? Has your family heard about this flap? I didn't think Paige had guts enough to mention it at home."

"I let it out myself," Katie admitted. "I told my mom what was going on to protect myself from a fate worse than debt . . . going out to lunch with Paige Whitman."

Lisa whistled softly. "That must have been a pretty scene."

"Tearjerker," Katie assured her lightly. "All we needed was violin music. This was followed by other classic scenes . . . lover's quarrel featuring mother and stepfather, and tender scene between father and wronged daughter. Once everybody chose up sides, the cold war was on. Breakfast at the North Pole with icy glances and frigid civility all around the table. It's a wonder somebody didn't get frostbite in the crossfire."

"The words don't fit the music, Katie," Lisa told her. "You're talking serious stuff here."

"I'm talking serious stupidity," Katie said, dropping her lighthearted pose for a moment. "If everybody wants to take Paige's silly lie and blow it up into a Federal case, that's their problem, not mine. I refuse to creep around feeling guilty when I haven't done a single wrong thing."

"Okay," Sara said doubtfully. "If you can get away with it."

"Watch me!" Katie told her with a winning smile.

"I'm watching," Lisa said quietly as Mike Lynch turned the corner and approached.

He slowed as he saw Katie. "Hi beautiful!"

"Mind your manners," Lisa corrected him. "There are three of us here. Try that in the plural."

He laughed, "Point well taken, Conrad." Then, turning to Katie, "Walk you to class?"

"Why not?" Katie shrugged. "Thanks a lot," she told Lisa and Sara. "Both of you."

"What did they do?" Mike asked.

Katie shrugged. Might as well be up front about it. "They came early this morning to cheer me up."

Mike laughed. "That's a good one. What's next? Are they going to give you swimming lessons?"

Katie grinned but said nothing. He couldn't possibly be kidding like that if he'd heard the rumors about the two of them. She was right. He was as innocent of the whole mess as she was. It was the least she could do to stand by him publicly as well as in her heart.

In a way Paige was glad that no one else on the staff had come up with any new evidence about the cheating scandal. Ben didn't let up nagging at her about getting the story, but at least now he was nagging at everybody else as well as her. In the meantime they had a paper to get out. She enjoyed doing quiet detailed layout work with Laurie looking over her shoulder now.

The speech department caused a small but irritating flap. They turned in contest results written by hand. Jim typed them up for the printer, but when Paige took them down to be proofed in the department, a Mindy had strangely changed to Wendy and the sheet had to be done over.

"That's it," Ben said furiously. "Somebody in that department *has* to know how to type. That article is going to have to wait until the next issue. But make a copy of that sheet and put it in the speech box. If nobody yells Monday, we run it that way."

As she worked, Paige watched Ben from the corner of her eye. Why didn't she ever get tired of that relentless energy of his? He paced and shouted like a human volcano without ever letting up. Yet when the two of them were together, on their rare dates or stopping for food after covering an athletic event, he became quiet, the liveliest thing about him being those remarkable hazel eyes studying hers. She found herself smiling secretly. What a guy. What a bright, strange man. At closing time, when she glanced up to see him signaling her to stay, her heart leaped. Maybe he missed her, *too*, when they didn't get any time together.

"Wish I had my bike," he told her. "I'd give you a lift home."

"No problem," Paige said, wondering what other reason he had to ask her to stay.

"How do you think this is going to end?" he asked. Then hastily, "This business about Mike Lynch and your stepsister, I mean."

"Badly," Paige told him honestly. "Last night I talked to my dad — "

Ben didn't even let her finish. His challenge was swift and angry. "What's with your head, Whitman?"

"It was my neck I was saving," she told him. "Katie had heard what we were probing for and apparently told her mother I had started the rumor."

Ben groaned and slapped his forehead with the flat of his hand. "That's all we needed. Now we'll *never* get the hard facts."

"And we have to have them," Paige reminded him. "I told Dad all we had was circumstantial evidence. I've realized since then that it's worse than that . . . we only have hearsay."

Ben looked so disheartened that Paige laid her hand on his arm. "My dad also said that the truth would eventually come out."

Ben closed his hand over hers, then lightly pulled her against him. His voice sounded deep and resonant against her. "Eventually doesn't make deadlines," he said softly. "Did we think this was going to be so tough?"

"Pinning the story down?" Paige asked.

"That, too," he said. "I was really thinking about working with you every day and not having any time alone together."

"That, too," Paige echoed, her heart giving such a crazy jerk that she was surprised he didn't feel it through his sweater. He held her tight another minute and sighed. "When this crazy rumor business is over, we'll celebrate. Okay?"

She nodded, not really wanting to wait that long.

As Paige came up the drive, Jake Carson stepped out of the garage and called to her.

She paused and tugged her mind back from Ben Collins. Then Jake was there, looking down at her in his serious way. "How's it going?" he asked.

Paige shrugged. "So-so, I guess. How about you?"

His grin was sudden and brilliant and Paige caught her breath. This was crazy. How could she still be so attracted to this guy when Ben was so important to her? She'd called Katie fickle enough times. Was she fickle, too? Or was it natural for a girl to like two guys at once, especially two who were as different as Jake and Ben?

"Most ways, great," He said enthusiastically. "You know I've been coaching this basketball team for my friend, and I'm having the world's best time."

"I didn't know," Paige told him. "Are they winning?"

"Everything in sight." He frowned. "I'm surprised Katie didn't mention it."

"Katie and I don't talk much."

"Neither do Katie and *I*," he said, his expression changing swiftly. "You might say we parted in anger."

So what could she say in answer to *that*? Paige said nothing. He hesitated only a moment before asking, "Have you heard about some cheating going on at your school, the swim star Mike Lynch?"

Paige's heart did a flip-flop and not one of those wonderful kinds that it did for Ben.

"Why do you ask?" she countered.

"Katie was all upset about it the last night we went out," Jake told Paige. "I guess I gave her more good advice than she wanted to hear."

At Paige's questioning glance, he went on with a shrug. "I told her she must know who was doing it because team members *know* things like that." He grinned. "I also told her to stay away from Mike Lynch. She chose to interpret that as jealousy."

Paige waited. Was it possible that Katie hadn't told Jake that Paige had started the rumor? "That was good advice," Paige said finally. "About staying away from Mike Lynch, I mean. I'm not sure you're right about the whole team knowing it. If so, nobody's talking."

"Who's asking them?"

Paige winced. She had set that one up for herself. "Naturally the paper is looking into it," she said calmly.

"And is Mike cheating?"

"I really can't talk about it, Jake," she said, suddenly sick of the whole business and a little scared by the intense interest in his eyes. "The whole business is just on the edge of libel."

"Slander," he corrected her. "Libel has to be written down."

"Thank you, Mr. Attorney," she said, smiling in spite of herself. He *was* going to make a good lawyer. He even thought like her dad did.

"I'll take my fee in an answer," Jake told her. "If your news staff is looking into this, they have to have leads. Is Katie really the suspect?"

Paige felt herself flush under his eyes. He didn't even wait for her answer but immediately exploded angrily.

"Talk about *slander*. There's no way that girl would ever cheat for anybody, not even for herself."

"Don't yell at me," Paige said, suddenly angry at this explosion. "It's not *my* fault. I didn't start this story."

Jake fell silent, studying Paige. "Do *you* think Katie could be doing it?"

What had Judy called her? A world class bad liar? Paige dropped her eyes. "That's what *everybody* thinks!"

"And what do *you* think, Paige? Honestly."

Paige was silent and then picturing Katie in Jake's arms said, "She could be." She hated herself as the words came out.

Paige was startled to have Jake grasp her arms hard. "Listen to me, Paige," he said rapidly. "You're wrong. They're wrong. I'd put my life on their being wrong. You've got to *do* something. Katie is not just another knockout pretty girl, she has the makings of a great athlete. A mess like this could ruin her chances permanently. And she *is* your sister."

Stepsister, Paige corrected him silently.

"Maybe I should talk to that editor of yours, you know, the guy who was at Mrs. Whitman's party. What was his name? Collins?"

Before Paige could answer, she saw Jake

stiffen and look past her toward the street. She turned to see Katie step out of Mike Lynch's car. Katie stared up the drive at them, then turned her back to speak to Mike in the car.

"Well?" Paige said.

Jake said bitterly, "How can she *do* this?"

The expression on Jake's face was too painful to look at. Paige muttered something and fled into the house, leaving Jake watching Katie with mingled frustration and hurt.

Paige stopped in the kitchen, hoping Katie would go right on upstairs and change as usual. Instead, Katie came down the hall and slammed the kitchen door open.

Miss Aggie might have been there for all Katie seemed to care. She didn't even glance around the room but only stood in the door, her bright eyes flashing fury and her cheeks flaming with color. "What a witch you are! At it again, aren't you, Paige? It isn't enough that you start a nasty rumor at school and mess me up there. Oh, no. You have to try to mess me up with Jake, too."

Paige suddenly felt battered. This was too much. Ben, Jake, and now Katie all hammering at her.

"Shut up!" Paige shouted at her. "Nobody *has* to mess you up with Jake. He's got eyes. He saw you hanging onto Mike Lynch. Don't you think he can add two and two and get four?"

Katie cried out with rage. "I didn't . . ." she began. She was trembling. Her fists were clenched tightly as she came toward Paige. For a minute Paige retreated, actually afraid that Katie would hit her. But Paige didn't stop talking. She only raised her voice to drown Katie out.

"If you aren't doing it, you *know* who is," Paige told her. "Jake says the same thing. And knowing the cheater and protecting him is just as bad as doing it yourself."

Katie's eyes widened, showing white all around the shining blue. She stared at Paige a moment, gasped, then turned and fled.

CHAPTER 10

Katie ran down the hall, got halfway up the stairs, and stopped. From where she stood she could hear her mother and the younger girls playing together in Megan and Mary Emily's room upstairs. Megan's giggle was followed by the soft peal of Virginia Mae's laughter. Katie stood very still. Usually at this time of day her mother was downstairs wearing fresh makeup and an air of excitement. Katie often laughed to herself about it. Her mother acted like a teenager ready for her first date when it was time for Bill Whitman to come home for dinner.

But that had all stopped when Virginia Mae and Bill took sides with their own children on the swim team scandal. Although Katie wouldn't have given up her mother's support for the world, what it had done to Virginia Mae's marriage scared Katie.

Katie couldn't stand listening to them with her

own heart aching with anger and pain. Neither could she face that messy pig-pen of a room she shared with Paige, and she wasn't about to lock herself in the bathroom which was all there was left for her! She had *no* place to go, no way to escape Paige, who was very like a looming dark cloud, shutting off all the sunshine in her life.

Katie turned and pulled on the jacket that she had thrust into the hall closet in passing. She opened the front door stealthily and let herself out. She stood on the porch a minute with her hands jammed deep in her pockets. Then, without really having a plan, she started to walk. The cold air left her cheeks stinging. Since the park would at least give her shelter from the wind, she crossed at the corner and chose a bench that was backed by a giant oak tree.

She didn't want to think about what Paige had said but it wouldn't go away. It was almost as if Paige's words had been burned into her brain:

"If you aren't doing it, you know who is. Knowing the cheater and protecting him is just as bad as doing it yourself."

Paige was wrong. Katie didn't know anything about anyone cheating. *If* she was going to admit that Mike could be cheating, and that was the biggest *if* of all, she didn't have any idea who might be helping him. But even if she knew something like that was going on, what would she do about it?

"I don't want to think about it," she said aloud. "I just don't want to think about it at all."

She gasped at the sudden sound of soft laughter, and jumped to her feet. Jake, his jacket collar pulled up against the wind, was standing on the dead grass a few feet away, smiling at her.

"I've heard of people talking to the trees," he told her. "I just never saw it happen before."

Katie turned away. "I was talking to myself," she said hotly. Why did he have to come right now? She had missed him so much since their fight. But she didn't want to see him now when she felt about as strong as a cooked noodle.

"Getting any good answers?" he asked. Then he was there. His arms around her made her want to cry.

"Oh, Jake," she said, turning to him. "There *aren't* any answers."

With his arm around her shoulder, he led her back to the bench. "I don't know that," he said. "But then I haven't heard the questions."

When she didn't say anything for a moment, he spoke hesitantly. "Just say the word and I'll take off. I saw you cross the street as I left the house. Being a red-blooded American male, I followed my instincts."

She managed to smile at him. "Don't go away. I just couldn't take that place any more. I can't take this whole cheating business any more."

"No better, huh?"

Katie shook her head. "It just goes on and on. I wish that silly paper would print the rumor and get sued and have it over with."

"Ben Collins is too smart for that. He knows about libel."

"Then he better make Paige stop whipping up the gossip by asking everybody about Mike's grades."

"Paige is only doing her job," Jake told her.

Katie caught her breath angrily and jumped to her feet. "Naturally you'll defend Paige. The fact that she's ruining my life, trying to pin something false on me doesn't matter to you at all. Paige is *always* right."

Jake caught her arm and pulled her back down on the bench. "Lay off that, Katie. Paige didn't start this, but Ben Collins isn't going to let up until he gets the truth."

"And what if the truth is that *nobody's* cheating? How's he going to end it then? Print an article saying that everything everybody has heard about Mike Lynch and Katie Guthrie is wrong?"

"Ben would have pulled Paige off this story right away, if there hadn't been some evidence of funny stuff. You were telling that tree you didn't want to think about something. What is it, Katie? What can't you stand to think about?"

Jake's arm was warm around her shoulder and she relaxed against it. "Paige lit into me in the kitchen," Katie said sulkily. "She said protecting a cheater was as bad as being one. If anybody's cheating, I don't know it. But, Jake, even if I did, I don't know whether I could make myself squeal on one of my teammates." Her voice trailed off.

"That's a tough one," Jake agreed.

"And it just goes on and on," Katie said again, wearily.

"You know what I'm thinking," he said.

She nodded. She knew all right. He was thinking that if she was all that sure of Mike, she'd ask him. A car slowed in the street beyond them and turned up the Whitman drive. She got to her feet.

97

"That's Bill's car," she said. Then she smiled at him. "You're lots more fun to talk to than a tree."

He caught her close and kissed her gently. "That goes here, too. Remind me always to follow pretty girls."

By the time he walked her home, arm-in-arm, she could even face going back into that house again, which, in its way, was even colder than the wind outside.

The worst of it was how *polite* everyone was.

Hypocrites! Katie told herself angrily, I live in a nest of hypocrites. She would almost rather everyone yelled at each other the way she and Paige had that afternoon. But no! Her mother's smile was as starched as a crinoline petticoat, and her stepfather's conversation sounded strangely formal, as if it were something he had memorized to say in court.

She and Tuck escaped as soon as dessert was over on the excuse of homework. Tuck grumbled crossly as he followed her upstairs. "What a scene!" he said. "Straight out of a carnival sideshow. Step right up folks! Pay the nice gentleman in the striped suit and see Living Parents transformed into plastic mannequins overnight!"

"I'm scared," Katie admitted.

"We all are," Tuck said. "Them included. When's this stupid mess going to be cleaned up anyway?"

"What if there's nothing to clean up?" Katie asked. "It'll just go on and on."

He turned and stared at her thoughtfully. "Have you asked Mike Lynch about this story?"

The words wouldn't come. Jake . . . then Tuck.

"No," she said flatly. "I wouldn't think of insulting a friend."

"Not even for the sake of your family?" he asked.

She was glad he didn't wait for an answer, but turned into his room and shut the door behind him.

The weekend of the famous Saturday lunch came and went with the house exceptionally quiet and the meals unusually dull. Only the younger girls seemed to continue a normal pattern of life.

"I can hold my breath for forty-two seconds," Megan boasted over her Sunday night sandwich.

"Run your stopwatch, Tuck," Mary Emily commanded. "I bet I can hold mine longer than that."

Paige watched Mary Emily's cheeks puff up and her eyes begin to water, before she finally exploded and collapsed into laughter. "How did I do?" she asked the second she had breath enough to speak.

"Forty-two seconds exactly," Tuck said, snapping his watch shut.

"Wow!" Megan said, turning to thump Mary Emily. "Together we can hold our breath eighty-four seconds. I bet that's some kind of a record."

"I think it's a record that you added those numbers in your head," Tuck told her.

Paige set her plate and glass on the sink and went into the study to practice. Virginia Mae hadn't touched the piano since the night of the heart-to-heart talks. It was nice always to have the piano free to practice on, but not nice enough to make up for the misery in Paige's father's face.

How did kids come up with games like that, she wondered idly as she got out her music. In a way she felt as if she had been holding her breath ever since the night she and Ben heard about Mike Lynch cheating. They were no closer to proving anything now than they had been that night. How *was* this going to end?

CHAPTER 11

As Paige walked into the newspaper office, Carrie was trying to talk on the phone while Ben stood over her struggling to grab the receiver out of her hand.

"What's going on?" Paige whispered to Laurie, who was bent double over the layout table, laughing helplessly.

Laurie wiped a tear of laughter out of her eyes and shook her head. "Don't mind me. I think we're all about hysterical down here. We had just wrapped up the copy for the printer when the speech department called again. Remember Mindy who used to be Wendy? Now they claim they wrote Sandy on the list in the first place."

Paige giggled. "What's the matter with those people?"

Ben, overhearing her question, whirled on her. "All wind and no brainpower."

Jim grinned and asked quietly. "Is this what they mean when they claim to be spellbinding?"

Ben groaned and glared at him. "Everybody's a comic on Monday," he said. "They'd think we were pretty funny if we charged them staff time for every correction."

"At our wages, they'd never notice it," Carrie said, catching his words as she set down the phone. "And, Ben, it's rude to scream at someone in the middle of a flowery apology."

"I'll give them flowers," he threatened. "Okay, Paige. This is stupid but necessary. Carrie got this mystery person's supposedly correct name from the speech secretary. Check in the office to be sure such a student exists. If it checks out, make a copy of this list and take it down to the speech department. Make the woman initial one copy so she can't call back and raise a fuss again."

"Wait, wait," Laurie called. "While you're down there, I'd like one copy each of these three items. I forgot to tell Jim to carbon them for the file."

After Paige checked the name on the student roster, she realized she hadn't remembered to bring money out of petty cash for the copier. She found a dime in her book bag and copied the speech page and took it down. The speech secretary scratched her initials at the bottom of the list and handed it back, glaring. Ben had called this whole drill stupid but necessary. It was certainly stupid enough.

After getting a dollar changed in the office, Paige took Laurie's folder back to the machine.

When she lifted the flap of the copier, she realized someone had used the machine between her trips. She laid the sheet aside. Whoever had forgotten it would be back, probably before she was through with Laurie's stuff. She'd done that enough times herself to know how silly they'd feel when they missed it.

She stared idly at the machine while it flashed green, growled, and sent her copies through. After stacking them, she turned the abandoned copy over to lay it on the rubber flap. She didn't really read what was written on the paper, but her mind registered that it was a full sheet of copy divided into numbered units.

Five steps down the hall Paige's mind clicked almost audibly. The words she had read on the paper in the copier seemed to be printed a mile high in her mind.

That paper in the copier hadn't been just anything. It had been a test. The first question had asked something about the economic situation in Russia during the reign of Peter the Great. That was a history test.

She shook her head. But it had to be an old test for any teacher to be that careless about leaving it around. Then she froze, whirled, and went back to the copier, suddenly cold all over.

Just standing in front of the machine made her feel scared and somehow guilty. In case the owner of the paper should come up and see her there, she fished in her bag for more change while she studied the test. World History IV, Bruce Donnelly. Her heart began to thump wildly. Mr.

103

Donnelly taught the senior history section that Mike Lynch was in. The test was dated the following day.

Paige fumbled with the coin as she fitted it into the slot. She pressed the green square quickly, silently ordering the machine to move fast. The moment the copy slid into the chute she replaced the original on the machine and slid the copy into her notebook. If she ever needed to describe how a person felt with her pulse running out of control, she could do it now!

Her first instinct was to fly downstairs and show the test copy to Ben. Maybe he'd just explain it away. There could be a perfectly reasonable explanation. Several of the teachers had student assistants. Maybe Mr. Donnelly had sent one of his aides down to make copies, and he or she had just been careless.

She stood in the hall, indecisive. While she was using the copier she had been so sure that the owner of the paper was going to come up behind her any second. If she went down to the newspaper office now she would never know who had left that history test there. And whoever had left it wasn't going to come back if he (or she) saw her hanging around. The hall was not only *not* designed for surveillance, there wasn't even a convenient corner she could lurk behind.

She looked back at the copier thoughtfully. If she opened the auditorium door and stood just inside it, she could see the copier through the waist-high plate glass window in the outer office.

If anyone asked why she was there, she could always just die.

Once she got the heavy door open and stepped inside, she had to lean against the wall. She was damp with sweat, as if she had been running, and she was breathless with the cold worse than it had been before. She thought of Ben waiting downstairs for the speech department copy. Ben's impatience was legendary. She had taken more time than she expected, making the two trips to the copier. Any minute Ben could come striding up angrily to see what was keeping her. She had to take that chance.

A couple of senior girls went into the office together and leaned on the counter to get something from the office secretary. Neither of them even looked toward the copier. The assistant principal, Mrs. Foster, came out of her office carrying a briefcase. She put on a gray ultrasuede coat and wound a rose scarf around her neck and left.

Jennifer Bailey came down the hall with Tuck at her side. Paige drew back tighter against the wall, remembering wistfully when she and Tuck had been close enough that he had talked to her about Jennifer. That closeness was long gone, blown away by all her problems with Katie.

Katie.

Paige gripped the wall behind her. What if Katie was the person who came back to the copier for that test? She shoved the idea away, unable to deal with it.

She pushed back her sweater sleeve with one finger and groaned silently. It was almost closing time at the paper. Soon the swim team would be dismissed and come thundering through the hall.

She wouldn't have a chance of seeing who slipped in and out of the office if that happened!

When she thought about what a fit Ben was probably having downstairs, she wavered with doubt. If this turned out to be a completely wasted drill, he would never let her forget it. But she had gambled too much on this chance to give up now. She shifted her weight, changed position a little bit, and kept on watching.

Katie finished a lap and touched the end of the pool with her outstretched fingers. Mike Lynch was standing with Charlie Evans and a couple of the other guys at poolside. Mike winked at her and grinned as she inhaled for the return.

She smiled and pushed off. Mike made her feel sad. He was on her mind more than she wanted to admit. It was awful, absolutely terrible for a good, maybe even great, athlete like him to be accused of cheating. It could ruin him. She felt guilty every time she thought of him, and in debt, as if she owed him something.

Because all this time, none of it was his fault. It was only his bad luck to have been caught in the web of Paige's deceitful conniving. She wondered if the other members of the team felt the same way. They *had* to have heard the rumors. She watched to see if they treated Mike any differently from before. It was no good. Since he didn't really hang around with any of them but her, she couldn't see any difference at all.

Charlie had left, but Mike was still standing there when she finished the last lap. As she pulled up to sit on the edge of the pool, Mike squatted beside her. "You know I could watch you all day."

She laughed and tugged off her cap. "Problem, friend. I couldn't *swim* all day."

"Maybe I could think of something else for us to do," he told her. "I'd even settle for an hour at a time."

She read his approval in his face. She knew from the way his eyes smiled at hers and the way his lips moved that he liked her, everything about her. As if in answer to her thoughts, he reached over and flipped a curl back from her shoulder. "A few scattered minutes?" he asked, dropping his bid one more time.

She chuckled. "You know you are just a disgraceful flirt, Mike Lynch. Why waste your time on me? Haven't you gotten even a little tired of hearing me say no?"

"Not in that accent," he told her.

He was so easy to talk to. He liked her so much. Did she dare ask him what Jake and Tuck both had suggested? At the thought, she felt her breath come shorter. Why was she afraid? But why shouldn't she be? She remembered her own swift fury when Tuck had told her what was going around. Why should Mike be any less insulted than she had been?

But she *had* to ask him. After all, they were in this together, both of them had a lot to lose. She opened her mouth and was phrasing the question when the coach's whistle shattered the air and signaled to clear the pool.

Mike took her hand and pulled her to her feet. "Rise and shine, beautiful. I've got to dash."

Katie opened her mouth and then closed it. She

had been on the point of asking him to drive her home. There in the quiet of the car they could have talked. Maybe he could help her figure out some way to put a stop to all this nonsense. And why didn't *he* bring up the subject to her?

As she glanced past him, she saw Sara and Lisa waving from the seats way up in back. At least she wouldn't have to go straight home without a little extra fun. And anyway, what was the hurry? That was the most frustrating part of it all. There wasn't any hurry, she thought bitterly, not the way this was dragging on and on and on.

CHAPTER 12

Paige fought a rising sense of panic as the minutes slipped away and the huge building emptied of both people and sound. The phones had quit ringing in the administrative offices. The last counselor walked out with a student. When the big front door banged shut behind them, a hollow echo reverberated along the hall.

Was any of this going to make sense to Ben?

When she heard rapid footsteps approaching, she shrank against the wall, really expecting to see Ben turn the corner, striding in that angry way he did, frowning. But the figure that came into her line of vision was a shorter man, wearing a hooded warm-up with the school's name blazoned across the back. He walked to the office door so quickly that she didn't see his face. Only when he stopped in the doorway to look up and down the hall, did she realize it was Charlie Evans, one of the seniors on the swim team. After a moment he walked quickly to the copier and lifted the flap. He shoved the test sheet into his notebook without even looking at it and stepped back into the hall.

Paige hugged herself with excitement. If Charlie Evans was the one helping Mike, then she was out of it with Katie. Her relief was almost unbearable. And for Charlie to do it made some kind of crazy sense. Charlie was a senior, too, just as Mike was. Even though he was nothing like the star that Mike Lynch was, he was outstanding enough as a swimmer to get an athletic scholarship from a fairly good school if the team won All-Conference. He had a far stronger reason to help Mike cheat than Katie had ever had.

Swim practice was over. Paige heard the metal clanging of distant lockers being slammed shut. She was trapped. Within minutes the team members, whose laughter and voices she could already hear, would be surging by on their way out of school.

The boys on the team reached the front hall first. Charlie Evans waited as his teammates approached and fell into step with them. They were boisterous and loud, shoving each other and laughing at nothing. Some had pulled the hoods of their sweatshirts over their wet hair. Others, like Mike Lynch, were bareheaded with damp towels draped around their shoulders. The walls vibrated with their noise. A draft of cold air swept around Paige's ankles as they fanned the big front door, letting themselves out. The girls followed in a group with Katie and her friends, Lisa and Sara, bringing up the rear.

Paige caught her breath. Why was she always

freshly startled at how beautiful Katie was? It was ridiculous that with all the trouble and pain her stepsister had caused her, Paige found herself transfixed by Katie when she saw her like this. Katie glowed as if she were lit from inside. The smile she beamed toward Sara was brilliant. Paige, feeling lanky and graceless, looked away, unable to deal with her own inadequacy against a girl who glittered with such a vital, glamorous force.

The minute the hall was empty again, Paige left the auditorium and ran breathlessly downstairs. She paused in the doorway of the silent newspaper office. Ben was the only one left. He was standing with his back to her, staring out the window. He turned as she entered and looked at her quizzically. "Five more minutes and I was going to send out a St. Bernard dog. Where have you *been?*"

Before she could answer, he crossed to her. "Carrie went looking for you, but the speech department was locked up tight. I figured you had to come back for your coat."

Paige was at a loss for words. "I found something in the copier," she blurted out, handing him the test. "I stayed there hoping to see who came back for it."

He took the paper without looking at it and tilted his head at her. "I can't believe you! You've been spying on that copier all this time?"

She nodded. "Read what I handed you," she ordered.

He frowned as he read the first few lines of the test.

"Mike Lynch is in that history class," she told him.

He looked up quickly, his expression thoughtful. "You're sure?"

"I'm the one who worked through his schedule, remember?"

He studied the test paper another minute. "So did anyone ever pick up the original?" he asked.

Paige nodded again. "Charlie Evans. He came and got it just a minute or two before the rest of the swim team came down the hall."

"Did he act worried?"

She hesitated. "Maybe just careful not to be seen."

Ben turned, checked the rotary file on Jim's desk, and dialed a number. Paige felt herself begin to tremble as she listened to his half of the conversation.

"Mr. Donnelly? Ben Collins here. Paige Whitman and I need to see you for just a minute if it's all right." He paused. "I know it's late. This will only take a minute. No, it isn't anything I can ask over the phone. We'll be right up."

"I don't want to talk to him," Paige said. "How can I do this to Mike and Charlie?"

Ben caught her hand, ignoring her comment. "He said he was on his way out. We were lucky to catch him."

Ben hadn't exaggerated their luck. Mr. Donnelly was standing with his briefcase beside him outside the history room door. His overcoat was already buttoned, and he was pulling on brown leather gloves that matched the color of the scarf over his shoulders.

He glanced at Paige but he spoke to Ben. "What's up, Collins?" he asked.

Ben glanced down the empty hall and nodded toward Paige. "You know Paige Whitman?" When Donnelly nodded, Ben handed him the printed test and went on. "Paige found this and we thought you'd want to know about it."

Bruce Donnelly was a square-faced man of about forty. Paige had always thought him good looking in a bland, almost colorless way. His color deepened as he looked up from the test. He narrowed his eyes thoughtfully as he stared at Paige.

"Where did you find this, Miss Whitman?"

"It was under the flap of the copier outside the office," she told him.

"She also saw Charlie Evans come back for the original later," Ben said.

Paige paled. It was done.

"So you made this copy?" he asked.

She nodded, feeling the color rise in her cheeks.

"What use did you have for it?"

Paige caught her breath sharply, but her swift tug of fear was drowned out by a voice she knew was hers. "If I'd simply told you I saw a copy of your test for tomorrow, it would be my word against the word of whoever had the original."

Paige and Mr. Donnelly looked at each other steadily for a moment. Mr. Donnelly picked up his briefcase, opened it, and slid the test paper inside. "This is the second year Charlie has worked for me as a student assistant," he said, his tone expressionless. "He's always been very dependable. Certainly not usually this careless.

Thank you for bringing this to my attention. Is that it?"

"That's it," Ben said. Paige and the teacher exchanged another of those uncomfortable long glances. Then Ben took Paige's elbow and started off. "Have a good evening," he called back.

"Same," Mr. Donnelly said, still standing by his door.

They were all the way downstairs before either of them spoke again. "I feel awful," Paige admitted as Ben held her coat. "I had some crazy idea that the whole mess would be all over right there."

"It could be," Ben said quietly.

She looked up at him. "But you heard him. If Charlie Evans is his assistant, and if Charlie just left that test in the copier . . ."

Ben shook his head. "What did you expect Donnelly to do? He's been working with Charlie and owes him the loyalty of not jumping to conclusions. He barely knows you or he would have called you Paige. The ball's in his court now, and he knows it. We're into a waiting game."

"I could scream," Paige wailed. "I was so sure."

"You could still be right. Or you could be wrong. Hey, it was a good try."

Out in the parking lot, Ben stopped, then took Paige's hand and motioned her to follow him. He led her around to the back of the building and looked up. The security lights glowed dimly along the length of the building. The windows of the third second-story classroom from the end glowed brightly. Ben nodded and tightened his arm around Paige's shoulder.

"Donnelly's room," he told her. "I guess he wasn't in as much of a hurry as he thought he was."

He stood a minute staring into space, holding both her hands. "It could be tough, but we can't tell anyone about this."

"You mean I can't say anything about it to *anyone*?" Paige asked, aghast. The only person she would have mentioned it to anyway was her father. Every time they had a moment together since the night of the big blow-up, he had asked her how the investigation was coming along. And every time she really looked at him, she realized afresh what a burden it was to have this rupture between himself and Virginia Mae. His eyes showed the strain and his voice was deeper, sadder, as it had been during those lonely years after her mother's death.

"Nobody in the world," Ben said firmly. "If Donnelly sent him down to make copies for the whole class, you wasted your whole afternoon, and we're back on square one again."

Paige had always thought of herself as a private person. She had always been good at keeping secrets, both her own and those of other people. Hadn't she been hopelessly in love with Jake Carson for over a year before Katie found it out . . . too late for Paige? All of a sudden, she had lost the knack. The minute she saw her father's car following her up the back drive, she wanted to rush to him and tell him what had happened with Charlie Evans and the copier. Instead, she only waited for him. They walked to the house together with his arm around her shoulder. "What's up?" he asked after a glance at her face.

"Nothing," she said guiltily. "Why do you ask?"

He looked at her again, intently, then smiled. "You looked different somehow, excited." Then he shrugged. "Maybe I'm imagining it because I *want* this business about Katie and Mike cleared up so much. You will tell me if anything breaks?"

"You know I will," she said, hugging his arm tight as he reached for the back door. "I want it over as much as you do."

"Well, I doubt *that*!" he said without smiling.

She left him feeling very guilty. But she had told him the truth. As Ben had pointed out, nothing had broken, and raising her father's hopes only to have them dashed later was the worst thing she could possibly do.

Paige's second huge temptation to tell what she had seen happened very late that night, after she and Katie had both been asleep a long time.

Paige wakened slowly to someone whispering softly and tugging on the sleeve of her pajamas. As she pulled herself up and leaned on an elbow to look at Megan, she saw by the clock light that it was a little after midnight. Megan's usually smiling face was tight with concern as she shoved her tumbling red curls out of her face.

"What's the matter, honey?" Paige whispered. "Why aren't you asleep?"

"It's Mary Emily," Megan whispered. "Please come quick."

The word "quick" startled Paige to her feet. Before she and Megan reached the door, Katie was up, too. "What's wrong with Mary Emily?" she asked defensively, her voice probably more brusque than she meant it to be.

Megan began to whimper. "She cries," Megan said. "All the time she cries."

Katie shoved Paige aside and sped out the door. Paige followed with her arm around Megan. "How long has this been going on?" Paige asked. "Is she sick?"

"She's been funny a few days lately," Megan said. "She only started crying tonight."

They were at the door of the younger girls' room. With no light on, the furniture loomed only as rough shapes. Katie and Mary Emily were clearly visible, silhouetted by the outside light from the window. Katie was perched on Mary Emily's bed, holding her little sister in her arms. From Mary Emily's low, miserable sobbing and the way she caught her breath now and then in a sharp gasp, Paige realized she had been crying a long time. Katie was speaking to her sister so softly that it sounded almost as if she were crooning. Paige couldn't catch her words or what Mary Emily was trying to say between her sobs.

Katie glanced around. When she saw Paige in the doorway, she stiffened. "Go away," she whispered. "She's my sister. I'll take care of her."

Megan clung to Paige's hand as they stood in the door.

"Go away," Katie said again, bringing a fresh surge of sobs from Mary Emily. "This isn't a side-show, you know."

Paige stepped back into the hall and Megan

followed. "Katie will make her all right," Paige assured Megan. "Didn't Mary Emily tell you what was the matter?"

Megan shook her head, but she caught Paige tight around the waist. "Oh, Paige," she whispered. "I can't live without Mary Emily. She's my best friend ever in the whole world."

"You aren't losing her," Paige said, kneeling to hold the girl close. "She's yours forever. She's your sister."

"I'm afraid," Megan said.

Katie appeared in the doorway and motioned to Megan. "She's all right now," she told Megan. "But she wants to know if you'll sleep with her and her teddy."

Megan nodded and padded obediently back into her bedroom. Paige heard the girls' muffled voices and the creak of bed springs, then went back to the room she shared with Katie.

Katie had thrown herself on her bed. She lay stiffly on her back with her arms crossed under her head. Paige, unable to think of anything to say, crawled under her covers.

"That's a girl, Paige," Katie said furiously. "Just roll over and go back to sleep. What do you care that a little kid like that wakes up scared and heartbroken because of you?"

"Me?" Paige asked, sitting upright in astonishment.

"You!" Katie said angrily, turning to punch her pillow with a clenched fist. "Mary Emily may be only ten but she has eyes in her head and brains behind them, which is more than I can say for you."

"All right, Katie Summer," Paige said, her own anger rising. "Make sense instead of insults for a change."

Katie's brilliant eyes shone with fire as she leaned toward Paige. "She's crying because she doesn't want to lose Megan. She says your father is going to leave our mother just the way our dad did and take Megan with him."

"But that's crazy!" Paige cried.

"Is it that crazy? Your father and my mother have been angry strangers ever since they found out about this plot of yours against Mike Lynch and me. Mary Emily knows about divorce and she's scared."

"Divorce," Paige breathed. "That's crazy, wild."

"Is it *really*?" Katie asked sarcastically, turning her back on Paige. "Think about it, Miss Trouble-maker."

"Katie," Paige said. "Let me tell you something."

"Shut up," Katie said sharply, pulling the covers up over her ears. "Shut up or I'll scream and wake the whole house."

Paige sat on the side of her bed watching Katie. What if she just started to talk and told Katie what had happened at the copier that day? Katie would hear her whether she wanted to or not. Unless she decided to scream.

With Katie so upset and so impulsive anyway, Paige realized she didn't trust Katie *not* to scream. She sighed and lay down, trying to shove the word "divorce" out of her mind.

CHAPTER 13

Only a few minutes remained in Paige's last-period class when Molly Cavannah, who worked afternoons in the counselor's office, came to the door of the room. Paige's teacher walked over to Molly, listened to her whispered message, then took a folded note which she handed to Paige.

Paige, feeling every eye in the room watching her, nodded but didn't unfold the paper until the bell rang. There was a single line of typed copy. "Please report to Principal Gray's office immediately after your last class."

Paige's mind was filled with instant protests. She hadn't done anything to be called in for. She was due at the newspaper office. She had to get word to Ben that she would be late. But the note said "immediately" and just the word sent shivers of apprehension up Paige's spine. She gathered her books, still feeling curious eyes on her, and was one of the first to leave the room.

Ms. Gray's secretary looked up as Paige entered the outer office. "Hi, Paige. That was fast!" she said genially, marking a list that lay on her desk. "Just go right into the office. Ms. Gray will be right back."

The minute Paige was inside the office, she was seized by surge of hope. The secretary had marked her name off a list. Three chairs had been set facing Ms. Gray's desk with an extra chair beside her own. Why had she been so scared? This meeting probably had something to do with a student council committee.

Paige was trying to think what committee might need an unscheduled meeting like this when her hope was dashed. Ben Collins opened the door, looked at her, and crossed the room to take the chair next to hers.

"Interesting," he said in a whisper.

"Scary," she corrected him. His grin would have been more reassuring, if he hadn't had a pale line of tension around his mouth.

Ms. Gray came next, followed immediately by Charlie Evans and Mr. Donnelly, who closed the door behind him and took the chair beside Ms. Gray, facing the students.

Paige felt herself shrinking. Without glancing her way, Ben stirred and pressed his leg against hers for an instant.

Ms. Gray looked at each of them. "I think you all have some idea of why I called you here," she said quietly. "Some rather mysterious things have happened in the last twenty-four hours. We've come together to clear them up." She nodded to the history teacher. "Please start us off, Mr. Donnelly."

Charlie Evans, on Ben's right, stirred in his seat clasping and unclasping his hands.

Something about Mr. Donnelly's voice reminded Paige of her father. He spoke carefully, almost monotonously, the way her father did when he was trying to get a careful point made without emotion. "Before I start, I want to say that Charlie Evans has been a valuable assistant to me for the past two years. I have never had any reason to doubt his dependability."

Without looking his way, Paige could feel Charlie's rising tension. Tears were at the back of her eyes and she clenched her hands.

"However," Mr. Donnelly went on. "Last evening as I was leaving the building, Ben Collins and Paige Whitman called me on the phone, then came to my room, and handed me this." He withdrew the test copy Paige had made and laid it on Ms. Gray's desk.

"Where did you get this copy, Paige?" Ms. Gray asked.

"I made it on the copier in the outer office," Paige replied in a low voice.

"Why?"

Paige swallowed hard. "I found it there under the flap when I went to make copies for the paper."

"But why did you copy it? Why didn't you simply return it to Mr. Donnelly's office?" Ms. Gray persisted.

Paige felt the muscles of her throat tighten and looked at Ms. Gray helplessly. "Wouldn't that have been the obvious thing to do, Paige? You must have had some reason to make a copy and take it upstairs rather than just return it or dispose of it?"

Ben's voice was a harsh whisper. "Tell her."

"I wanted to see who would come and pick it up," Paige said, her hands shaking.

Charlie Evans sat stiffly in his chair, looking straight ahead.

"And why did it matter to you who picked it up?" Ms. Gray went on.

Paige tried to keep her voice steady. "There's a rumor being circulated by other schools in our conference that one of our athletes is being falsely qualified. All the members of the staff of the paper have spent a lot of time trying to disprove or prove the allegation. When I found a senior test paper due to be given the following day to a class which the accused athlete is in, I . . . I wanted to know who had left it there."

Paige felt as if Mr. Donnelly's eyes were probing right through her face into her brain. "Who picked up the paper from the copier, Paige?" he asked.

"Charlie Evans," she said, hearing her voice break.

"That's a lie," Charlie said fiercely.

"You had access to that test, Charlie," Mr. Donnelly reminded him. "Are you certain you didn't take it to the copier and leave it by mistake."

"Why should I do that?" Then, under his teacher's steady glance. "No, I didn't."

"I'm asking you a very important question,

Charlie. Did you make copies of this or any other test for that class and make them available to another student?"

"No, I did not," Charlie said flatly.

Mr. Donnelly sighed. "The evidence points another way, Charlie. Last night, after Ben and Paige left, I prepared and duplicated a totally different test covering the same material. I gave the new test today. I graded the papers almost immediately. All members of the class had scores within their normal range of error except one. That student gave for the new test the correct answers for the test I did *not* give. Would you like to change your reply, Charlie?"

Charlie Evans shrunk in his seat and sat silent a moment, staring at the toes of his shoes. "Yes, sir," he said quietly. "I did supply that test to another student."

"And others before it?"

Charlie nodded.

"And have you been providing the same kind of help to Mike Lynch in other courses?"

"When I could," Charlie said. Then hotly. "It was for the team. We can't make All-Conference without Lynch. . . ."

"Thank you, Charlie," Ms. Gray said. "If you will please step into the outer office and wait for me there."

In spite of all she had been through about this scandal, Paige still ached for Charlie as he crossed the room stiffly and let himself out. And strangely, she felt even sorrier for Mr. Donnelly. He seemed grayer, older, all of a sudden, as if much of his life had been drained from him by this betrayal of trust.

"Now you two," Ms. Gray said, her tone a little angry. "Why did you have to put everyone through all this? Why didn't you just report this rumor to someone in authority when you first heard it?"

Mr. Donnelly roused himself and shook his head. "Be fair to these kids, Ms. Gray. There wasn't any way they could do that unless they had some evidence to show. Ben was behaving like a real newspaper editor," he glanced at Paige. "With a new reporter with her head on her shoulders. The important thing is to decide how to handle this problem."

Ms. Gray stared at him, clearly aghast. "But Mr. Donnelly, you know we have a set of long established administrative guidelines."

He nodded. "Those guidelines don't say anything about headlines and exposés in the school paper," Mr. Donnelly pointed out.

"No!" she exclaimed, turning a little pale. "We can't have that. We *really* can't have that!"

"Even though you never would have broken this thing without these two?" Mr. Donnelly pointed out. "There's a matter of honorable debt involved."

Ms. Gray looked from Paige to Ben helplessly for a moment before flattening both hands on the desk. The she smiled ruefully. "They say the Romans shot messengers who brought bad news. I'm going to have to do a version of that. I hate doing it, but I have to shoot down your big story."

"No!" Ben cried out.

"Yes," Mr. Donnelly nodded. "You can't run headlines exposing those boys in print. You are clever enough to think of a lot of options, I'm sure. Maybe you could run a big feature giving the new roster of the team. Don't you think that will be as sensational as a smear headline?"

Ben was silent for a moment. "I guess it really will," he conceded grudgingly. "You're right. It really will."

Ms. Gray rose. "I am going to make a request that I want you to understand as an order. Certain administrative steps have to be taken with both boys and their parents. Please don't let what happened here become general knowledge until we have had an opportunity to take those steps."

Paige nodded, but Ben rose and frowned. "Can you give us any idea of when that will be?"

Ms. Gray looked at Mr. Donnelly and then at the clock on her wall. "A series of appointments have already been set up starting at five this afternoon," she said. Then, turning to Ben, "Tomorrow morning. I am sure I can trust your discretion."

Mr. Donnell smiled sadly. "Ben's not going to blow this big story by making it general property before the paper's out."

"And you, Paige?" Ms. Gray asked.

"I don't care about the story," she said. "I just want this over."

Paige passed with Ben through the outer office and couldn't bring herself to look at Charlie Evans. But she was so conscious of his misery that she trembled inside. She had just done one of the most difficult things she'd ever had to do,

126

and she hurt for herself and for Charlie and Mike.

"It's about time you two managed to drag yourselves down here," Laurie scolded as Ben and Paige walked into the news office. "Paige, did you ever get that list corrected from the speech department? And you, Ben . . . did anybody cover anything for the sports page this week?"

Paige fumbled the speech list out of her book bag with cold hands. "I'm really sorry, Laurie," she said. "I got held up yesterday and forgot all about it."

"We'll dock your pay," Laurie said, grinning at her and fitting the initialed sheet into the printer's packet. "That winds up my day."

"Don't worry about the sports page, Laurie," Ben said. "Paige and I will throw something together. Maybe we can even come up with a story that will knock your eyes out. Right, Paige?"

Jim and Carrie followed Laurie out after only a few moments. The minute Paige and Ben were alone, Paige turned to him. "I don't know exactly what she meant by administrative steps."

"That's when the school authorities set their feet down hard on Mike and Charlie's necks. For certain they are off the team as of right now. They may possibly suspend both boys from school."

"But they're both seniors!" Paige cried.

"Yeah," Ben said quietly. "Nobody can say they didn't ask for it, so why don't I feel better about this?"

"Is it because you lost the big scoop?" she asked.

He shook his head. "I must be going soft. I'm

127

really sorry for those two stupid jocks."

"And Mr. Donnelly," Paige added.

He nodded. "The only one I can be glad for is Katie Guthrie. I'm really relieved that it didn't turn out to be your sister who was carrying Mike Lynch."

"Stepsister," Paige corrected him absently.

"*Stepsister!*" she shouted. "Oh, Ben, we have to tell my folks. We can't let Katie walk in on this tomorrow without any warning at all. No matter what they think in the office, some sort of crazy story about this will be all over school by ten o'clock. Katie's going to lay the blame smack on me unless she knows how it happened."

Ben frowned and checked his watch. "Okay, let's do this job fast. Make a list of all the facts and angles we can use on a full-page spread on the swim team. There's the article Ms. Gray mentioned, of course. Then we have to catch the coaches and interview them about the guys taking their slots. We can run stats on them." He paused. "We should get that thrown together in time to be at your place when the clan gathers for the evening feeding."

Paige stared at him, suddenly seeing the faces of her family in her mind. "Oh Ben," she cried. "I don't know if I can really face Katie with all this."

He leaned and pressed his lips to her forehead. "You did a first-class job of facing things so far," he reminded her. "You're probably good for one more."

CHAPTER 14

When the hands of the clock reached ten until six, Paige couldn't stand it any more. "Ben, we have to go. We're far enough along on this. I'm going to get home late for dinner as it is."

He frowned. "Give me just one more minute."

He pulled over the phone and dialed. Paige whirled when she heard him speak. "Tuck, is that you?" he asked.

Paige stood listening to Ben's part of the conversation with her stepbrother. "Is Mr. Whitman in yet? Not yet, huh. Do me a favor, will you?"

Paige listened to Ben explain to Tuck that they were running late, but that the two of them would be along as quickly as possible. Then she heard him add, "That's right, the two of us."

Ben turned from the phone and raised his eyebrows at Paige. "How can a guy be so polite that he sounds rude?" he asked with amazement. "That's a real knack."

"It's an old southern secret," Paige told Ben. "But what has Tuck Guthrie got against me?"

"You're on the wrong side of the Cold War," she said, putting the last of the stats by Jim's typewriter.

He studied her face. "Have you dared to keep something big about your private life secret from me, Paige Whitman?" he asked in a bantering tone of insult.

If he had asked the question any other way, Paige might not have been able to deal with it. As it was, she could laugh. "You see before you a woman of true mystery," she told him. "Come on, look this display over and tell me what you think."

Katie went into the girls' locker room to dress for swim practice without checking the bulletin board. To her amazement, the usually crowded, noisy room was empty. As she stood trying to figure out what was going on, one of the other girls came in, slammed her locker open, and started taking off her swimsuit.

"What's up?" Katie asked. "Aren't you going to swim? Where is everybody?"

"Who knows?" the girl asked crossly. "As you see, I jumped the gun and was clear to the gym door before I saw the sign saying practice was canceled."

"Canceled," Katie said. "That's crazy." She frowned at the thought. With the schedule as hot and heavy as it was this time in the season, nothing short of a catastrophe would force the coaches to cancel a practice.

"He *could* have told us yesterday," the other swimmer said, pulling on her jeans.

"Maybe something's wrong with the plumbing," Katie suggested.

"I didn't hear anybody in there working. More likely something's wrong with coach's head," the girl said. "I could have been flirting with my guy over at Paddy's if I had known we weren't going to swim!"

Paddy's. Katie shrugged. If she was lucky, maybe some of her crowd would be at Paddy's having after-school Cokes. Back at her locker she exchanged her swim bag for her backpack of books and homework. As she ran down the front steps of the school, she saw Mike Lynch's car pulling out of the parking lot and hailed him.

He waved at her but didn't slow down or stop.

She stared after him, Not my day! she told herself lightly, shrugging, and started down the street.

It wasn't her day at Paddy's either. The place was half full and the noise level deafening when she walked in. A couple of people waved at her, but none of her own crowd was there. And strangely, none of the other swimmers were there either. She shook her head when someone beckoned her to join a table and went back outside. It wouldn't hurt her to go straight home one afternoon.

Going home early turned out to be relaxing. With Paige off at her newspaper office, Katie had the room to herself for a change. She played her favorite cassettes without having to use her earphones, brushed Binker until the cat crackled with

131

static electricity, and read a chapter ahead in English. By five-thirty she realized she would never survive until dinner without at least a glass of milk.

Miss Aggie was basting a chicken that smelled so good that Katie groaned. "You're destroying me, Miss Aggie," she wailed. "Never mind the others. Let's eat. I'm starving."

"You and your brother." Miss Aggie laughed. "I've been fighting him off this bird for a half hour."

"Where *is* Tuck?" Katie asked, pulling a bowl of vegetables out of the refrigerator. "Matter of fact, where's everybody? This house is like a tomb."

"Megan and Mary Emily have jumped another jean size and your mother has them out shopping. Tuck's friend was here after school for a while, what a nice girl! I guess he took Scarlett out after Jennifer left for home."

Katie munched celery and carrot sticks and looked over the morning paper, still on Bill Whitman's chair. She tried to concentrate on what she was reading, but her mind kept going back to the canceled swim practice and how much of a hurry Mike had been in. Could any of it have something to do with Paige and her vicious rumor? It seemed very strange.

Tuck came in the back door, his curly hair blown every which way from running with the dog. His face glowed and he looked as happy as Katie had ever seen him. As he hung the leash on its hook the phone rang. He caught it on the first peal.

Katie watched his face with astonishment. The smile left his face within an instant, to be replaced by an annoyed scowl. His usual relaxed drawl turned curt even though his words were civil enough. After telling the caller he'd give the message, he slammed the phone down angrily.

Miss Aggie stared at him a moment, then went back to her work. "What was that about?" Katie asked.

"Who knows?" he said, dropping onto a chair. "I mean I really don't like that guy."

"Ed Thomas?" Katie asked, guessing that Jennifer Bailey's other boy friend was giving Tuck a hard time again.

"Ben Collins," Tuck said, shaking his head. "He asked me to tell Bill that he and Paige would be a little late getting home."

"He's coming *here*?" Katie asked, leaping to her feet without even realizing she had done it.

"It sure sounded like that," Tuck said. "If he thinks he can come in here and expect any welcome from any of us . . ."

Katie shoved the vegetable bowl back into the refrigerator. "What a nerve he has!"

"He's Paige's friend," Miss Aggie pointed out mildly.

"That's right. And he's not mine," Katie told her thoughtfully. "I'm going back upstairs. Don't call me until he's gone. I don't trust myself around that guy."

Katie felt Miss Aggie looking after her with a puzzled stare but didn't care. As far as that went, she didn't trust herself around Paige anymore either.

At a little after six, Ben and Paige had done all they could do until they talked to the swim coach.

"That's it," Ben said. "Are you sure you want me to go home with you? You have a perfect right to go it alone."

Paige smiled at him. "I need more backup than just my dad."

"But he understands what has been going on?" Ben asked.

"He believed what I told him. That's the next best thing. I don't think anybody *really* understands how a rumor like that gets going."

Paige had never gotten over loving to ride with Ben on his moped. She loved the way he grinned into her face as he fastened her safety helmet under her chin and tilted the bike to help her on.

Never mind that the wind blazed against her cheeks and her nose was running. She liked pressing against Ben's firm back, clinging desperately with her arms tight across his chest. She liked the roar of the sensitive machine twisting perilously through traffic, dipping and swaying like a wild thing through the maze of cars. Maybe she liked it the best when he stopped and the motor gasped to silence. Then he always caught her arms with his gloved hands, holding her tightly for a minute.

When he brought the moped to a stop at the end of the drive, Paige saw her father's car through the garage windows and a felt a sudden panic. Ben, sensitive to her change of mood, tried to reassure her. "It won't be all that bad," he told her, his low voice vibrating through her jacket.

"That's a promise?" she whispered against his back.

Miss Aggie was tossing salad in a big crystal bowl as Paige let Ben into the kitchen. Ben groaned and grinned at Miss Aggie. "Bottle that smell and you'll make a million."

Miss Aggie chuckled. "I might even make it if I bottled my gravy. How are you, Ben?"

"Cleaner this time," he pointed out, reminding her of the time he and Paige had destroyed her kitchen floor with enough mud to plant a garden.

"Dad in the living room?" Paige asked.

Miss Aggie nodded. "Everybody else is upstairs."

Paige's father rose to shake hands with Ben. "Tuck gave me your message, Ben. Thanks for calling." His expression was guardedly eager. "Anything new on the cheating scandal?"

"Dad!" Paige cried, flying into his arms without thinking. With her head tight against his chest she spoke, having trouble keeping her voice level. "It's over, Dad. It's all over."

Bill Whitman motioned Ben to a chair and looked down at Paige. "And Katie's cleared." He said it as a statement with only the faintest shadow of doubt in his voice.

"Totally," Ben told him. He hesitated. "You know, Mr. Whitman, what we have to tell you is still top secret stuff. But Paige felt . . ."

"Dad, Mike Lynch *was* cheating. Katie has to

know so she doesn't walk into the talk that's bound to be all over school tomorrow."

Paige's father was silent for a moment. "Then you came to tell Katie as well as me."

"And Virginia Mae," Paige added. Did she *really* care about Katie?

Mr. Whitman looked thoughtful a moment, seemed to recover, and turned to Ben. "Like a cold drink, Ben? Coffee?" he asked. "I need to call the other women down here."

"I'm fine," Ben said, looking a little nervous suddenly. The minute her father crossed the hall to go upstairs, Ben reached for Paige's hand. His flesh was cold and a little damp, and she tightened her other hand around his.

"Cold hands," she said, smiling up at him.

"That beats cold feet any day," he said, grinning at her.

"I have those for both of us," Paige admitted.

Katie heard Ben's deep voice from downstairs as he greeted Bill Whitman. She rose angrily and shut the bedroom door. A lot of nerve that boy had coming in with Paige when the two of them had practically destroyed this family. "Home-wrecker," she whispered fiercely at the closed door.

Katie's mother was across the hall, having come in with the younger girls in an explosion of giggles and laughter and crackling paper bags. She knew what was going on in Megan and Mary Emily's room from having done the same thing so many times herself. Half the fun of shopping was coming home and trying things on again in front of your own mirror.

"That's wonderful!" she heard her mother say. "Now try the pink top with them."

The footsteps in the hall caught Katie off guard. If dinner was being served, her stepfather would simply call. But instead he was upstairs, rapping softly on Megan and Mary Emily's door. Katie, standing just inside her own door, strained to hear his voice.

"Virginia Mae," he called, his tone formal, as it had been all the time recently when he spoke to her mother. "If Megan and Mary Emily can spare you, we have a guest downstairs."

A guest, Katie thought angrily. Why didn't he come right out and say who it was so her mother could tell him to forget it?

Instead, a whispered conference took place in the hall and Katie heard her name before he rapped on her door.

Katie caught her breath deeply before opening it.

Her mother's face was expressionless. "Katie, your father wants us both downstairs a minute. Please come."

Katie looked at her, at the strain on her face, at her eyes which were sad instead of glowing as they used to be.

"Thank you very much," Katie said formally. "I really don't want to come."

Her mother didn't get a chance to respond. Bill Whitman spoke too quickly. "I'm sorry, Katie, but I have to insist. Please come downstairs with your mother and me."

"I don't like Ben Collins," Katie said hotly. "I don't want to see him or listen to anything he has to say."

"All of us do a great number of things we don't want to do in this life, Katie Summer," her stepfather said firmly. "I'm afraid this is something you *have* to do."

Katie felt a sweep of icy fear. What had happened? Had Ben and Paige managed to frame her so that she and Mike couldn't prove their innocence of those dreadful charges?

All this time her mother hadn't spoken. Why didn't she help her? Why didn't she tell Bill Whitman that Katie didn't have to go through any more agony at the hands of that awful daughter of his?

Instead, her mother reached out, took Katie's hand, and urged her forward. "Bill's right," she said quietly. "Come along, Katie, do as your father asks."

Katie stiffened. Stepfather, she corrected in her mind without daring to say it. But her mother's grasp was firm and her face so pleading that Katie had no choice.

CHAPTER 15

Katie almost balked again when she crossed the downstairs hall with her mother and stepfather to see Paige and Ben standing a little apart. They were both visibly self-conscious. Paige looked different somehow, standing there with Ben. Usually she just looked tall and gawky and skinny to Katie. When she was with Ben, her height seemed graceful, and instead of skinny, her long fine-boned body looked lithe and willowy.

Katie remembered that Paige's mother had been described to her as "candle slim." Even the phrase was romantic. While Katie wouldn't trade her well-formed sleek athlete's body for anything, she felt an instant thrust of jealousy. To someone who could stand her, Paige might seem candle slim, too.

Paige and Ben had obviously been talking quietly to each other. When Paige looked up at Ben, her dark hair fell in shiny waves over her collar. Even though her neck was plainly too long for any creature except a giraffe, when she held her head at that angle, it looked regal and wonderfully elegant.

She isn't elegant, Katie reminded herself furiously. No matter how she looks, she's mean and hateful and destructive. And I'm not going to listen to any of the lies Paige and her boyfriend are going to tell Bill!

Virginia Mae was her usual gracious, hospitable self. She crossed to Ben, shook hands with him, and said it was nice to see him again. Ben nodded, glanced at Katie and quickly away, and turned to Paige.

"Sorry to break in on your evening this way, but Paige and I . . ."

Paige put her hand on Ben's arm and broke in. "I wish everybody would sit down," she said. "I have something I want to tell you."

Katie took a chair away from the others. I'm here, she told herself crossly, but that doesn't mean I want to have any part of this.

Paige sat very straight, her hands tightly together in her lap. "What Ben and I have to tell you is not for anyone but all of you . . . for now, but we wanted you to know. This scandal about cheating which has been so awful is finally solved."

Paige told the story swiftly from the start, with a minimum of words.

"And that's when I started checking with people who attended classes with Mike Lynch," Paige explained. "It was as much to clear his name as anything else."

"This rumor about Katie," Virginia Mae asked. "How did that start?"

"Nobody really knows," Ben told her. "We figure it just rose because Mike and Katie were good friends."

"We *are* good friends," Katie said flatly, not letting him get away with that. He glanced at her, then went on. "Everyone Paige talked to agreed that Mike wasn't carrying his weight in class work. Then we got stalled."

"But I gather that's over now?" Paige's father asked hopefully.

Paige nodded, and tried to smile. "You've always told me not to depend on the long arm of coincidence, Dad, but it really struck this time." She told him about finding the test in the copier and waiting in the dark of the auditorium to see who came to pick it up.

Katie stared at her in disbelief. Paige must have been skulking there like some low-life spy when she had passed with the swim team the day before. What a crummy thing to do!

"Charlie Evans came for the test," Paige finished simply. "I took it to Ben and we took it to the teacher who would be giving it . . . Mr. Donnelly."

"When did this all happen?" Mr. Whitman broke in.

"Yesterday," Paige told him. "Ben and I have just lived through the longest night and the longest day of either of our lives. Donnelly was stiff about it, telling us Charlie Evans had been a dependable teacher assistant for a long time."

141

"Who is this Charlie Evans?" Virginia Mae asked, obviously a little confused.

"One of the guys on the swim team," Paige told her.

"One of the *best* high school swimmers in Philadelphia." Katie corrected her without even glancing her way.

"We didn't know any more until this afternoon after school," Paige told her father. "I got a note to report to the principal's office. Ben came in right after me and then Mr. Donnelly and Charlie Evans. In the end Charlie admitted he had been getting tests and answers for Mike Lynch all year and helping him any way he could."

Virginia Mae sat back with a sigh. "Then Katie's completely cleared! Oh, Katie . . ." she said, turning to her.

Katie couldn't meet her glance. This was wrong, all wrong. "Charlie Evans was lying," she said hotly. "He was getting that stuff for himself. Mike wouldn't cheat. I know he wouldn't."

"I'm afraid that won't hold," Ben told her. "Charlie's not even in that class and Mike is. Mr. Donnelly switched tests. Mike put down the answers to the copied test instead of the one he was given in class."

Katie held herself tightly, fighting the sudden rush of hot tears behind her eyes. Not Mike. It couldn't be.

"What did this boy say? What was his explanation for what he was doing?" Mr. Whitman asked, his tone wondering.

"School spirit," Paige told him. "He said the

school couldn't make All-Conference unless Mike stayed on the team."

"Any means to an end," Mr. Whitman said quietly. "What a sad story. Is that true, Katie?"

His question caught Katie off guard. "I guess it is; Mike is our star swimmer," she said.

Ben shook his head. "That's all over. Mike and Charlie and their parents were coming in for conferences when we left Ms. Gray's office. We will run the new swim team roster tomorrow. That's why Paige wanted Katie to know about it tonight . . . so she wouldn't be shocked when the news hit."

Katie stared at him, seeing the empty locker room, the cancellation notice on the gym door, and Mike speeding out of the parking lot without having time for a word with her.

She covered her face with her hands for a moment, then rose and fled upstairs, the sound of her sobbing audible in the silent room. Virginia Mae rose to start after her. Then she paused and leaned to take Paige's face in her hands. "Forgive me, Paige," she whispered. "I should have known better." She laid her hand briefly on her husband's shoulder. He caught it and held it a moment before she walked swiftly out to follow Katie upstairs.

Paige sat frozen. Why was Katie so upset? Wasn't she *glad* to be cleared of the awful charges? Katie was just overemotional. Strangely, as she asked herself this, Paige remembered Mr. Donnelly's face as he had sat in the office after

143

Charlie was sent out. He had looked bleak and betrayed, as if the ashes of his dead trust in Charlie had wiped the color from his face. Breaking a rule of honor didn't end with the disgrace and unhappiness of the person who did it. It was like a stone thrown into water, the disturbance fanning out to bring unhappiness to everyone who had been loyal to and trusted that person.

Ben and her father were still talking, discussing the possible course that the school administration would take against the athletes. Then Ben rose, and Paige felt his hand on her shoulder and looked up.

He grinned crookedly down at her. "It's time for me to shove off. Sorry we ran your evening late, Mr. Whitman."

"I'm grateful to have this mess over," Paige's father said fervently. "Stay and eat with us. We'd like to have you."

Ben shook his head. "Thanks anyway. I'll buzz off."

He took Paige's hand and pulled her to her feet. "Come see me safely through the kitchen," he told her. "I may need protection from Miss Aggie for wrecking her meal."

"Never had a bath of hot gravy?" Paige asked. "Might be fun."

"You try it first and check it out for me," he told her, grinning back at her father.

When she stood by the moped, watching him fasten his helmet, he looked down at her. "Now, that wasn't so bad, was it?"

"Yeah, it was," she said. "But it's over now."

"For us, maybe," he said, leaning to touch his

lips to hers for a warm moment. "But not for your sister. She took a hard one on this."

He's more sensitive to Katie then I can ever be, Paige thought.

And once again, she said "stepsister" in her mind.

Paige helped Miss Aggie get the slightly wilted meal on the table. Megan and Mary Emily tumbled down the stairs on the first call, both of them obviously feeling splendid in new jeans with matching tops. Tuck, right behind them, stopped by Paige a little awkwardly. "Mom told me what happened. What a mess."

"It's over," Paige said, not wanting to talk to him about it. She didn't want to talk to anyone about it ever again, she realized. This had been the worst of all the problems she'd had with Katie since her father's marriage.

Every other time she had been angry or hurt and done something that was the same as asking for what she got in the end. It didn't make any sense that this time, when she was trying so hard to get along, something had to come in from left field and cause more agony than she would ever have thought of causing on her own.

Mary Emily and Megan forgot their new clothes to elbow each other wildly when Virginia Mae and Paige's father came in hand-in-hand. "Katie's not feeling very well," Virginia Mae told Miss Aggie. "If you don't mind fixing her a tray, I'll take it up to her later."

Miss Aggie nodded and removed Katie's place setting before leaving the family alone.

"My chicken is chewy," Megan announced,

tugging desperately at the skin on her chicken leg.

"Mine fights back, too," Mary Emily told her. "I'm going to kill it by drowning it in gravy."

Paige, still numb from the day and evening past, listened to the younger girls tease and her father's glowing plans for a celebration dinner for the whole family. She wondered if Katie would ever be able to accept the fact that her good friend was a proven cheater. Would Katie even see Mike Lynch again? Only if the administration let him come back and finish his senior year. She was so deep in her own thoughts that she didn't realize her dinner plate had been replaced by a piece of Miss Aggie's famous cheese-topped carrot cake.

"Mom," Mary Emily said suddenly, in a bright tone that Paige recognized as daring. "Megan and I want to know something."

"Oh?" Virginia Mae said, a bite of cake balanced on her fork. "What's that?"

Mary Emily collapsed into wild giggles and punched Megan. Megan caught her breath as a bright flush of color reddened her face, making her pale freckles stand out like polka dots. "We want to know when we will be old enough to make out at the table."

Virginia Mae's eyes grew round. "Megan! What a thing to say."

"It's true," Megan insisted.

Mary Emily chimed in. "It *is* true. You and Dad have been holding hands and staring at each other all this whole meal," Mary Emily told her defensively. "That's what they call making out, isn't it, Tuck?"

Tuck chuckled and glanced at his mother. "Not exactly. And probably they had another term for it in the olden days, Mary Emily."

"Olden days, my foot," Paige's father said, pretending to be insulted. "Yes, we were holding hands or whatever you want to call it. As to your question, you little monsters, you can do it at the table when you're old enough to have your own impudent kid call you on it."

Until that next day at school, Katie didn't realize what a really *big* favor Paige had done her by giving her advance warning of Mike and Charlie's disgrace. The invisible grapevine was already humming by the time Katie arrived for her first class. By noon Katie's neck was sore from holding her head stiff and trying to ignore the whispers around her. Lisa and Sara greeted her wide-eyed. "Did you know about this before today?" they both asked the minute she set her salad down. She nodded and made a big business of opening her milk container.

Sara, who was always quick to read Katie's mood, dropped the questioning and spoke to Lisa in her most serious tone. "This whole business reminds me of Chinese food," she said soberly. "You know, sweet and sour something."

"Sweet and sour dummies," Lisa said helpfully.

"Maybe," Sara agreed. "The sweet part is that Katie is clean, as we knew she was. The sour part is how hard it is to believe that such a neat guy as Mike could be so stupid."

"He doesn't have a patent on that," Lisa reminded her. "Every gossip-hungry jerk who repeated Paige's nasty rumors about Katie is in the same boat."

Katie felt a bite of crisp lettuce catch in her throat. She thought of Paige's face, pale and nervous, in the living room the night before. She heard Ben saying quietly, "That's why Paige wanted Katie to know about it tonight . . . so she wouldn't be shocked when the news hit."

Now who was being the bad sport?

Katie said, finally getting the lettuce down, "Paige didn't start that story. I'm pretty sure she believed it when she heard it, but I honestly don't think she started it."

Lisa stared at her in disbelief. "Am I hearing you stand up for Paige Whitman after all the stuff she has done to you?"

Katie nodded. Then she grinned. "I don't have to let her take the rap for things she *didn't* do, she'll get raps enough for things she *does* do."

Lisa laughed softly. "Aren't you carrying this business of being a good sport to a ridiculous length?"

Katie shook her blonde head. "Good sports don't come in good, better, and best, like mattresses or something. You're a good sport or you're not . . . just like that."

They ate in silence for a moment. Katie knew that each of them was thinking about Mike Lynch. She knew it was the most painful for her. But that was nobody's business but her own.

Katie saw Jake standing by the garage when she came in from school that afternoon. She didn't want to talk to him. She already knew too well how he felt about Mike Lynch.

When he called out and waved at her, she just waved back and kept walking toward the door.

"Katie," he said urgently, coming down the drive double speed. "Wait up. I want to talk to you."

Since it was more awkward to get away than it was to stay, she stopped for him, hugging her books against her chest as if they could shield her from the words she didn't want to hear.

Once Jake was there right in front of her, he suddenly looked self-conscious. "I heard about Mike Lynch and wanted to tell you I'm sorry," he said after a minute.

"Sure, Jake," Katie answered bitterly.

Her tone made Jake angry. He flushed and his face got a hard look. "Sure, Katie," he echoed. "Decide what I think without listening to me! What kind of a louse do you take me for? I *am* sorry, both for Mike and for you. It's worse on him, of course, but it's got to be miserable seeing somebody you like in such a rotten hole."

Katie looked at him. Maybe he did understand, at least a little. She nodded. "I feel awful," she admitted. "It hurts even to think about it and I can't think about anything else."

Jake took Katie's books, laid one arm across her shoulders, and started up the drive with her. She was glad he couldn't see her face and know how hard it was for her to hold back her tears.

"Mike's really a decent guy, Jake," Katie told him. "I don't know what happened inside him to make him do this, but believe me, he's a decent, nice guy who made one big mistake. It's such a waste. He's so talented. Yet he's never going to be able to live this down."

Jake's tone was thoughtful. "Yeah," he said. "It's scary how long you have to live with a bad decision. And all of us make them." His arm tightened around Katie's shoulder. "I'm just so glad you were completely cleared."

Katie tightened instantly. "You *knew* I wasn't cheating. *Didn't you?*"

"I *knew* that. And I was just as sure that Paige wasn't trying to do you in." When Katie was silent, he looked down into her face. "That's right, isn't it?"

"Maybe this time," she said a little sullenly. She wasn't about to tell Jake how she really felt about Paige and her involvement in the scandal. That would only get her another lecture on what a great girl her stepsister was. Let Jake think what he wanted to, she wasn't going to be foolish enough to trust Paige about anything . . . *ever*. Just because Paige was in the clear this time didn't mean that tomorrow wasn't another day.

They were at the door. Anything she said would have been drowned out by Scarlett's loud barking welcome anyway. Katie turned to Jake and reached for her books. "Thanks, Jake," she said softly.

He lifted her chin and looked into her face a long moment. "You mean a lot to me, Katie," he said softly. "You know that, don't you?" When he kissed her, gently and for a long time, as if he never wanted to pull away, she felt closer to him then she had ever felt to anyone in her whole life.

150

She clung to him only a moment before going inside.

Megan and Mary Emily tried in vain to talk Paige's father into taking them to a place for the celebration dinner where they could wear their new jeans. "Not this time," he insisted. "I am going to get all my beautiful family togged up in their best and show them off in style."

So now Paige looked through her side of the closet in despair, then glanced over to Katie's neatly pressed, color coordinated wardrobe. It was disgusting. First the shirts, divided by color, pink, lavendar, yellow. Skirts were separated the same way, and after that dresses.

"The only thing that girl doesn't file is her teeth!" Paige told herself crossly, pulling out a navy dress her father had helped her pick out for his law firm's party the Christmas before. She shoved her hand hard down the skirt in hopes that would take the wrinkles out. When it didn't, she sighed and took it downstairs to press. Katie would wear something that glowed with color, that set off her sparkling eyes and shining hair. Maybe Paige would be lucky and get a seat behind a potted palm.

On what was supposed to be the festive night, the waiter led the family past the orchestra and straight to a long able by the window which was marked "reserved." As it turned out, Paige thought, nobody would have noticed if she had worn a gunny sack. The Guthries were like lamps that cast everyone else in shadow. Only Megan, with her flaming red hair, held her own with their good looks.

Bill Whitman turned to Tuck the minute they were seated. "You realize that we are the envy of every other man in this room, don't you?"

When Tuck looked at him quizzically, Bill Whitman laughed. "Okay. Then *I* am the envy of every other *father* in this room. No one ever had a more wonderful family than ours." He put his hand over Virginia Mae's.

Paige hoped he wouldn't go on and on like that, talking about his "one big happy family." But he looked down the table, his eyes dwelling a moment on each of them.

"This is a special night," he reminded them. "We've all come through a very tough time together. But we've weathered that crisis and it's all behind us. Surely this marks the end of our period of misunderstandings. I'd like to propose a toast to a whole new era of happiness."

Paige lifted her glass with the others. Without meaning to, she glanced at Katie. Paige's eyes were held by Katie's unwavering look. There was no mistaking what Katie was silently saying. I don't like you, and I don't trust you . . . and I never will.

Paige looked away thinking, How can my father be so wrong? How can we ever be one big happy family? It was a question that went unanswered. Was there an answer?

When their parents go away, a party Katie gives gets totally out of hand. Read Stepsisters #4, SISTERS IN CHARGE.